WHAT REMAINS WHEN THE STARS BURN OUT

P.L. McMILLAN

Front & back cover image by Waking Of Sky Tree.
Book design by Molly Collins.
Formatting by Molly Collins.
Interior illustrations by P.L. McMillan

First printing edition 2022.

https://www.plmcmillan.com/

Dedicated with much love to Matt

CONTENTS

Foreword

Most readers have individual preferences when it pertains to imbibing their horror.

Some like theirs shaken, others stirred. Some like theirs on the rocks, others neat. But then there are those who leap across the bar, snatch the bottle, slam it straight to their lips and knock it back—liquid dread dribbling down their chins.

If the latter sounds like you, then you've come to the right canteen.

Whether with "Godmouth," "Buzzkill," "The Space Between," or any of the horror cocktails in this collection, you'll find that P.L. McMillan doesn't waste any time with her macabre mixology. No tonic water. No fruity syrups. No aromatic bitters. However, she won't overlook salt—but it's only for packing into the gaping wound she's just ripped in your gut with the violent slash of a butcher knife when you were too busy guzzling.

I took my first swig of McMillan's Finest® a couple years ago. In fact, I found it almost completely by surprise when casually sampling the local horror brewing in Colorado with *Terror at 5280*, a showcase of Colorado writers. The ghost story "Left Behind" left me so drunk with dread that I immediately reached out to P.L., begging for more. I was hooked—and she only further supported me in my cravings. One after another, I chugged down whatever story P.L. McMillan sent my way. And even after reading this collection, I'm still looking for my next fix.

But perhaps I've mischaracterized her writing. While P.L. might be Canadian, her stories are far more potent than even the strongest Special Reserve Whisky from Crown Royal. They're closer to something like, well, absinthe.

Indulging in P.L.'s elixirs will take you places beyond your wildest imaginings. One sip will thrust you before megalithic structures jutting from white-capped ocean waves. Another swallow will push you into geographic anomalies breaking through the boundaries of space and time. And if you dare drink further, you'll find yourself jammed in a cryogenic capsule shooting across the galaxy to distant alien worlds.

So, it's time to wet your whistle with McMillan's Finest®. But first, we must remove the taste of all those bottom-shelf beverages you've been wasting your money on. Here, take this one. P.L. has fittingly named this concoction "Sanitize."

Bottoms up!

—Solomon Forse
Writing from Doc Holliday's Saloon
Glenwood Springs, Colorado
26 February 2022

SANITIZE

My eyes hurt from being so wide for so long, as I stared, unseeing, at my computer screen.

I had already washed my hands. I had already scrubbed down my desk with one of the sanitizing wipes I kept in the bottom drawer. My stomach tightened, twisted, roiled. I stared, yet could take nothing in. The computer screen was just a blur.

I had already washed my hands, I could still smell the soap. I had already wiped my desk, I could still smell the chemicals. My palms tingled. My eyes flicked down, escaping my control for a moment. Maybe I let them. My whole head felt fuzzy and my scalp was tingling now. I looked over my keyboard, over my hands which lay poised over top the keys, over the still glistening surface of my desk, over the mouse that sat beside my right hand, over to the corner of my desk where Jordan had sat as he blathered on and on about some report he'd wanted me to start before sneezing so wetly that I had physically seen the specks of internal Jordan juice spray out onto my desk.

What kind of barbarian didn't cover their mouth when they sneezed?

He'd laughed and apologized and I had kept my calm face on, waited until he left, then wiped down everything, then washed my hands, once, twice, three times in the bathroom – smiling at Carol as she entered, pissed, then only briefly rinsed her hands under water without soap. I made sure to use twice the amount of paper towels to open the washroom door.

That meant I was clean. I had washed my hands. I had sanitized my desk.

My traitorous brain asked me; what about your clothes?

I was suddenly very nauseous.

I looked at the time displayed on my computer screen. 3:51.

I opened a browser and began typing in "can germs survive on clothing" and forced myself to close it.

I looked down again. My hands were shaking over the keyboard, just slightly. My face felt hot, but my body was cold. I looked farther down, to the bottom drawer where my sanitizer wipes were hidden. Would they damage fabric if I were to wipe them over the shirt I was wearing?

I could hear my own breathing, ragged and harsh. I sucked in a breath and held it. Could Lee hear my racing, thunderous heart through the cubicle wall we shared? I forced my eyes back to the computer screen and tried, in vain, to focus on the report I had been working on when Jordan had disrupted my day.

Caught in the white noise cycle that my brain refused to leave, I found myself leaving the office before even realizing I had decided to flee. My mind whipped around and around: germs on my clothes, in my hair, my face, how far could a human sneeze spread, how much could it coat?

My phone rang when I was three blocks away, just entering the little park I sometimes ate lunch in. It was Sanjay. I slipped past a group of school kids, roughhousing in the middle of the path, and found that my favourite bench beneath the old poplar tree was empty. I sat. I answered my phone.

"Sanjay," I said, a part of me hoped he could hear the tremble in my voice, hear how close I was to crying, so that he would know how serious this situation was.

"Babe, what's up? You sound upset?"

"Jordan, that asshole. He sneezed all over me. I mean all over me, I had to leave work —"

It all got out of control when I said it out loud and my voice cracked. I clenched my free hand into a tight fist to stop its trembling.

"Take a deep breath, Paige. You're okay. You're going to be fine," he said.

I could tell he was annoyed. He never understood. He used to take me seriously, when we started dating two years ago, but now he just fazed me out.

"Listen, I was calling because my mother is going to be in town —"

"I think I should go home and wash my clothes. I think I should shower too, you know, just in case?"

He sighed. Loudly, deliberately. He wanted me to know he thought I was being silly.

"Aren't you afraid your boss is going to get mad at you for skipping out early? This is what? The third time this month? Doesn't he notice?"

"I —"

Had I left early three times this month? I looked at my watch. 4:18. It wasn't really early. I got off at five usually anyway. It was only an hour.

"Do you think I'm okay?"

"With your boss? I don't know, hun. You shouldn't be leaving early so often. I know germs freak you —"

"No, I mean about the fucking sneeze. It got on me, I know it did."

Another dramatic sigh. I realized I was biting my thumb-nail. If the germs were on my hand, then I'd just put them in my mouth.

Isn't the tissue of your mouth more susceptible to absorbing toxic material? Something about being a mucus membrane of some kind? my brain whispered.

"You washed your hands, right? Then you're fine. Humans have immune systems for a reason."

I opened my mouth to confirm. Then stopped. Had I washed my hands? I tried to reel in my memories, recount my actions from when Jordan sneezed to when I ended up here on this bench. My thoughts whipped away from me, it was like trying to grab a hold of a wet bar of soap.

"I can't remember. I don't think I did, I don't remember doing it." My heart was racing again.

I looked down at my treacherous hand as it lay, clenched on my thigh. It was tingling again. Why hadn't I washed it?

"You did, babe. You definitely washed your hands, you're always washing your hands." He laughed, such an easy-going sound.

I stared at my fist as it pressed into my thigh. If there were germs on my hand, wasn't I spreading it to my leg? I jerked my hand off my thigh and placed it on the cold metal bench seat instead.

"I didn't," I breathed into the phone. "I don't think I washed my hands. Why didn't I wash my hands? I need to get home, but if I touch my steering wheel, I'll have to sanitize the inside of my car and my keys too."

"Paige, listen to me."

White, sharp pain sliced through the storm inside my mind.

"Babe? Paige? Are you okay? What happened?"

I hadn't realized that I'd cried out in that moment. Everything seemed to freeze as I unfurled my fingers from where they'd wrapped around the edge of the metal bench. All sounds filtered away, even Sanjay's voice in my ear. The park faded away, lost in the tunnel vision I had on my right hand. There was the tiniest spot of crimson on my middle finger. Just above the middle crease.

"I have to go," I gasped.

I didn't hear his response. I hung up the phone, still staring at my finger.

I'd cut myself on the bench. I looked at the dark green metal slats. In some places, the paint had chipped away, revealing rusted metal. Was the underneath as rusted as – tetanus shot, when did I have one? I had to have had one, right? – digging through my purse with my left hand – hand sanitizer would help? Or was simple soap and water best? – that pain in my jaw, could it be lockjaw already or from my clenching it?

I was out of the park, my finger stinging as I rubbed hand sanitizer over it. I wouldn't run. I felt people's eyes on me and could only imagine what I must look like. My eyes were stinging as sweat ran down my forehead. I raised my arm up so I could rub at my eyes with my shirt sleeve.

Now the germs are in your eyes. Did you forget? Jordan sneezed all over you, my mind said.

I couldn't hold back the sob that exploded from my throat. I didn't stop trembling the whole way home. To break through the whirling frenzy, I began to plan out my steps. Over and over again, like a mantra.

Get home. Strip. Clothes in washing machine. Shower. Clean finger. Bandage. Sanitize car. Sanitize car keys. Over again. Home. Strip. Washing machine. Shower. Clean. Bandage.

Sanitize. Sanitize. Sanitize.

That's what got me home.

I could ignore the hot flashes dancing across my skin, I could ignore the way my limbs were shaking, I could ignore the taste of copper on my tongue. I could just concentrate on my mantra and I would get home.

My phone was ringing. Loudly. Right next to my ear.

My eyelids scraped like sandpaper as I opened them. I stared up at a darkened ceiling. I shivered on the cold floor, straightening my aching body. My phone went silent, then immediately began to ring again. I pushed myself up into a sitting position. I was in my front hall, still dressed in the clothes I'd worn to work that day. My purse was lying by my feet, its contents spilled out everywhere. Only a faint light filtered in from the front door's window, a false mellow light likely from the streetlight in front of my house – which meant night had fallen.

The ringing stopped, then resumed. I picked it up, flipping it over to reveal a newly cracked screen. The digital brightness blinded me but I managed to answer it.

"Paige? Where the hell have you been? I've been calling all night!"

It was hard to concentrate on Sanjay's voice. My head throbbed so hard that I could hear it. A low rush of tide that filled my ears with static, then receded with a wave of pain. I reached up, fumbled, got the light switch, clenching my eyes shut against the enveloping light.

"Paige? Paige? This isn't funny!"

"Sanjay, I think I'm really sick," I rasped.

"I can't believe this," he said. "You need to start your sessions with Dr. Cage again. You've regressed so much since you quit therapy, I just can't handle it. You know I'm stressed with this big project I've been working on."

I put my hand down to lean on it and immediately recoiled. There, just beside me on the floor, pooled lukewarm brownish, chunky bile. I retched a bit at the sight of it.

"— you have to know you're being irrational right? I know you're better when I'm at home, but I can't leave work just because you might have a panic attack. I told you this morning I might have to pull an all-nighter with the team.

You have to get in control of yourself for once, be more self-aware —"

"I have to go, I'm so sorry, Sanjay," I said and hung up.

I raised my right hand with the intention of pressing it to my forehead to check for fever but froze. There was a small amount of dried, crusty blood on my palm and fingers and where the cut was, my skin had discoloured into streaks of green, purple, yellow and was mottled with tiny bumps. The colouring and bumps ran around the middle joint of my middle finger like a ghastly ring, and streaked downwards to the middle of my palm. I pressed my left index finger against the palm of my right hand. The bumps were hard and firm, my skin was tender and hot. Touching it, even gently, caused a prickle of pain to dance over the entirety of my hand.

I stumbled to my feet, rushing to the kitchen. I turned on the sink, all the way on hot, and scrubbed my hands beneath the water – dousing them in disinfectant hand soap. When I dried them with a dish towel, I saw that the rash had spread to my wrist. It had moved so fast. How was that possible? The angry buboes on my arm were twice the size as those on my hand and finger. I grabbed my phone and dialled.

"911, what is your emergency?"

I spent the time it took for the paramedics to get to my house rubbing hand sanitizer all over my hand and arm. The panic subsided, replaced by a terrible chill and a strange rushing feeling, like an internal undercurrent, in my head. I couldn't remember what I'd said to the dispatcher. I had no sense of time between the end of the call to when my door-bell rang.

Holding my right arm out from me to avoid it touching

any other part of my body, I opened my front door. A man and a woman, dressed in blue uniforms and solemn expressions, stood on my stoop.

"Ma'am? You called in for assistance?" the man asked.

"It's my arm!" I held it out, the dark discolouration had crept up my forearm to the crook of my elbow in jagged trails.

They stepped across the threshold and into my narrow hall. The woman glanced down briefly but no reaction crossed her face.

"I'm Rick and this is Emma," the man said, setting his bag down. "Can you tell us what's happened?"

"Yes, I – this afternoon Jordan sneezed on me and – but I don't know if that matters. I went to a nearby park and cut my hand on the bench. It was a metal bench, I think it was rusty. I can't remember when I had my last tetanus shot," I started.

Emma held a hand up.

"Calm down, ma'am. Why don't you sit down? How about in the kitchen?" She nodded at the open doorway.

"I am pretty sure it was rusty and I rubbed hand sanitizer on my hand but I don't know if that would have helped. I don't think it did," I continued in a rush, leading the way into the kitchen and sitting at one of the chairs that encircled the small wooden table by the fridge. "I think I passed out when I got home. I woke up on the floor. And I saw – I saw this!"

I laid my arm out on the table so they could see. Emma sat across from me, Rick sat by my side.

He took a blood pressure cuff from his bag. "I'm going to go ahead and take your blood pressure, okay?"

"Ma'am, are you currently on any prescription drugs?

Have you missed any doses today, maybe?" Emma asked.

"No, I'm not on anything. I think maybe I need anti-biotics? I think I need to be taken to the hospital!"

I couldn't understand why they weren't examining my arm. The infection or whatever it was had widened to the point that it covered the width of my forearm and the entirety of my palm. Maybe this was a regular reaction, something they'd seen before?

"Look at me, ma'am," Rick said and I did, squinting at the bright pen light he held at my eye level, flashing it in and out of my vision. "Dilation seems normal."

"What about this? You need to examine my arm!" My voice was rising in volume and pitch.

"Your arm? I thought you said you cut your hand?" Emma said.

"I – I did! I did! But it's spreading! It's in my arm now!"

"What's in your arm, ma'am?" Rick had leaned back to pack his light and blood pressure cuff away; he wasn't even looking at me.

Wasn't even glancing at my arm.

"This!" I gestured at my limb.

Emma sighed and the two paramedics exchanged a look.

"Ma'am," Rick said and reached out, taking my arm in both of his hands before I could pull it out of his reach. "Your arm looks fine. Now if you did cut it on that bench, I would recommend going to your primary care doctor tomorrow and they'll check when your last tetanus shot was and all that."

"That's not true, there is something wrong with me! Look – look at my arm!"

He sighed and forced a smile.

"There's nothing wrong with your arm, ma'am," he said. "Look for yourself."

He lifted my arm off the table, squeezing it slightly in his hands. At the pressure, several of the larger bumps on my forearm burst, spilling a clear viscous material speckled with rust-coloured flecks. Instantly I could smell the faintest citrusy scent, it was almost pleasant.

I jerked my arm away from him, the burst bumps stinging. My mouth gaped as I watched the paramedic lean back in my kitchen chair and run a hand through his thick blonde hair. I could see the thick liquid glistening on his head. The red flecks caught the light and seemed to spark a brighter crimson.

"It's a really awful thing to waste our time. There are real emergencies out there that require our attention," Emma said, standing. "Come on, Rick."

I looked back at him. He was staring at his hands with a wide-eyed look of bewilderment. His partner walked past him, unaware, and stopped in the hallway.

"Rick?" she said.

I looked at his head. Where the goopy discharge used to be were now holes. I thought I could hear – just faintly – a sound much like frying meat. Then he screamed. He kicked back, flipping himself and my chair back onto the kitchen floor and then he rolled onto his side, seizing. His partner scrambled to his side, pushing him onto his back, struggling to pull his clawed hands from his face.

It was insane how fast it happened. The skin on his head slumped downwards, pulling away from his skull like jello, sliding down the sides of his face, and revealing bone. His eyes, naked orbs, spun in their sockets as he continued to scream. Globs of skin dropped from his hands, dripping like a fleshy rain until they went limp, lying in their own pools of gore on my kitchen floor.

The room filled with a strange sweet smell. Emma shrieked when she saw the naked skull where his face should have been. His feet beat a soft tempo on the floor before going still. She scooted away from him, shaking, then she looked at me. I tore my eyes away from his skull, his unseeing but staring eyeballs, the pools of pink flesh that haloed his head and lay in puddles around his skeletal hands.

"What the hell? What the hell did you do?" she shrieked and lunged at me.

I tried to dodge her grasp, I tried to jerk my right arm away from her, but she was faster. She grabbed my arms, tightly, her long nails digging viciously into my flesh. Dozens of plump boils burst along my arm, coating her left hand and wrist, but she didn't seem to notice – or see.

There was so much of it, it was dripping off my arm in great slimy dollops to land with small slaps on the floor. I gagged, trying to pull away.

"What is wrong with you? What did you do to him?" she screamed.

"I don't know – it's the rash! Don't you see? You have to wash your hand! You have to get it off!" I stood so fast, I almost knocked her to the floor.

I ripped my left arm free and used it to grab her wrist, pulling her to the sink. She flinched away from me, slamming against the counter, and her hands flew to cover her mouth as she looked at me with such a frightened expression that I froze. We stood perfectly still for a moment, locked together in fear. I watched the clear fluid sink into the flesh on her hand. Her skin wobbled, then sagged lower and lower before it dropped to the floor with a thick sound.

Her eyes followed its plummet and then she jerked her hands away from her face, holding them up to eye level. Side by side, she examined her whole hand and the one reduced to glistening bone. I thought she would have opened her mouth to scream except that she must have gotten some of the liquid on her lips, her left cheek, her chin. The bottom half of her face dripped away from her skull, joining the rest of the jiggling flesh on the floor. With a low keening sound slipping from her throat, Emma's eyes rolled back into her head and she slumped to the floor.

Then the kitchen was quiet except for the humming of the fridge and the soft susurrus of flesh being softened, separated, stolen from bone.

My legs threatened to give out so I sunk to my knees, wrapping my left arm around myself while holding the right as far from me as I could. It had spread. While I'd been watching Emma's face fall from her skull, the disease or the infection – whatever it was – had crept up my upper arm. It had spread far enough to disappear beneath the rolled-up sleeve of my shirt.

With trembling fingers, I pulled my collar down and revealed more tainted flesh across my chest and bordering the base of my neck. The bumps that had burst closed already, grown larger, full again to the brim with the clear, thick, poisonous brine flecked with crimson. I moaned and let my head fall back with a thud against the counter, tears threatening.

Somewhere in the hall, my phone began to ring again.

If I called the CDC, what would they do to me? Quarantine me. Keep me locked up until they figured out how to help me or I died. Dissect me. Use me to create biological weapons.

What if you don't die? Would that be worse? My mind whimpered and I shivered in answer.

Still, I couldn't let it spread any further. I had to see a doctor.

I planned it out in steps. Clean the infected flesh. Wrap it up in bandages to avoid leakage of any kind. Drive to the ER. Explain it all, explain everything.

I ignored the phone and whispered my mantra out loud as I walked around the cooling bodies on my kitchen floor.

Clean. Wrap. Drive. Explain.

Clean. Wrap. Drive. Explain.

The sterile smell of chemicals that saturated the air at St. Joseph's Medical Center helped steady my nerves. The bored looking nurse in pink scrubs behind the desk did not.

"And you say you got some kind of an infection from a park bench?" she repeated in a monotone voice for the fifth time.

"Please, you have to help me! It's not normal! Paramedics came to my house and when they touched it – when they —" I knew crying wasn't helping, wasn't making me seem reasonable at all, but my nerves were fully shot through.

"Can you quiet down, miss?" The nurse sighed. "You're being disruptive."

"You have to get a doctor to see me now! I can feel it leaking! I don't know if the bandages are thick enough, it's all I —"

"Fill this out. A doctor will see you in a while." She shoved a clipboard across the counter at me.

"It has to be now! The infection is spreading!"

"You have to fill this out, miss. Everyone does. Please sit down and return it once it's done."

She swivelled in her seat to turn her back to me and began to peck away at her laptop. I took the clipboard in my uninfected hand and gingerly made my way to an empty seat as far from anyone else as I could.

Though I had only just wrapped my arm in bandages, damp patches were appearing in the cloth. When I sat, I felt one of the larger abscesses pop and the thick, warm liquid trailed down my ribcage and onto my belly. Everywhere was the smell of lemons.

I stared down at the form. I was right-handed and now my right hand lay swaddled in an inch of bandage. I put the back of my left hand against my forehead.

No fever. No aches in my joints. No shivers or cold flashes. No sore throat or cough.

Even the infected skin felt the same as the rest. There was nothing to show that I was sick, possibly dying, except for the marks, except for the toxic growths that laced my limbs like weapons.

I jerked out of my thoughts with a snap at the sound of a scream and looked around the waiting room, my heart in my throat. A heavily pregnant woman had just walked up to the front desk, three children orbiting her legs as she did. She shooed them away as she spoke to the nurse and they dashed into the waiting room like snotty comets. I grew tense, watching them circle the seats and the other people waiting to be seen. I shrunk into myself, back into the chair, curling my legs under it.

One of them, a little girl with long pigtails, ran past me with an ear-piercing giggle. Then her brother raced after her and tripped over his own feet, landing right in front of me. He began to howl. The dozen other people in the waiting room looked up from their phones, their magazines, the TV mounted to the ceiling. They looked at him and then set their stares on me. My skin prickled.

They're wondering who that cold woman is, letting the kid cry and cry, and not offering to help, my mind whispered.

They stared. I stood. The mother turned and watched me. I stepped over her son, stumbling in my haste to get far from him. She made a clucking noise on her tongue and began to waddle over. They were all staring. All staring as she stumbled, off-balance due to her magnificently bulging belly, and fell against my right side. Out of instinct, I reached out to steady her even as I felt every single pustule pop along my arm, shoulder, and side. The bandages soaked through. My clothes were slimy. I stumbled away from her with a shriek, falling to the floor in front of the nurse's desk. As I scrambled, I left a glistening trail along the floor.

"What is your problem, lady?" the pregnant woman asked as she knelt awkwardly and yanked her son to his feet, leaving sticky handprints on his arms.

The nurse was at my side. She reached down and grabbed my arm.

"Miss, if you're going to cause a fuss, I'm going to have to call security and you don't want that, do you?"

She gripped my forearm, oblivious to the rivulets of ooze squeezing out from between her fingers.

"Oh God, you have to wash your hands now! You have to get it off! It'll kill you!"

I felt lost, swept away, completely out of control. The nurse dropped my arm and raised her hand between our faces, spreading her fingers apart.

"There's nothing there. Look! There's nothing there. Do you understand that? What kind of medication are you supposed to be on, anyway?" she said as ribbons of clear, liquid infection stretched between her fingers.

"What's going on here, Angela?"

The nurse and I looked up. A man in mint-coloured scrubs stood in front of us.

"Nothing, Dr. Tanaka —"

"They're going to die! You have to listen to me! Her, and her, and – and the kid! It's all over my body and if it gets on you —"

"Now, now. How about we let Angela take care of everyone out here and I take a look at you, okay?" he said with a smile, completely unfazed.

"Doctor, I —" The nurse started and then stopped when he flashed her a look.

She stood and made her way to check on the pregnant woman. The doctor watched me stand shakily and then led me around the front desk, down the hall, and into an examination room. I was babbling. I couldn't stop. My words flowed over the stoic doctor like rain drops, unnoticed.

"Take a seat, Miss…?"

"Paige MacDonald, but —"

"Medications?" He pulled on some gloves and set to work, unravelling the sodden bandages from my arm, letting them fall into the biohazard disposal bin by the counter.

"None, none at all. I'm not crazy, it's right there!" I gestured at the raw, gaping holes that ran the length of my arms – ruination from the pregnant woman's fall against me.

He hummed to himself, turning my arm this way and that.

"And you think you have an infection because you cut your finger? Are you experiencing any fever? Aches? Sore throat?"

"This! This is the evidence right here, right here!"

"Do you have someone we can call?" he said, staring at my arm and yet not seeing anything.

The screams started. A part of me was waiting for them this whole time so I didn't even flinch. Dr. Tanaka did, jerking upright, ramrod straight and eyes wide.

"Just wait here, alright? Just wait – wait one moment." He was out the door before I could say a single thing.

I didn't wait. It was clear to me that he didn't understand what was going on. The paramedics didn't take me seriously, the nurse hadn't, and now the doctor. The more people who didn't take me seriously, the more people died.

The screaming ended abruptly, but I could hear a panicked babble of conversation. I slid off the examination bed and slipped into the hall, running past the mob who crowded around the three prone figures on the floor – two adult-sized and one child-sized. They didn't even see me escape the hospital, clutching my right arm to my chest, and dripping ichor the whole way out.

I drove home, hardly aware of the streets I took, my head was crowded with thoughts of what steps I should take next. Nothing seemed plausible. Everything seemed hopeless.

I didn't even notice the front door had been unlocked, until I was already in the front hall. It wasn't until I saw Sanjay standing in our kitchen, his face pale and drawn as he stared down at the two bodies lying on the floor, did I realize I had parked next to his cheery red sedan when I'd gotten home.

"Paige," he said, breathlessly. "Oh, Paige. What the hell happened here?"

"You have to get out of here, Sanjay! You have to leave. It's not safe. You can't be near me, I'm sick!"

He turned haunted eyes to meet mine.

"You have to go, you have to get far away from me. Please, Sanjay." I pressed myself against the wall, wishing I could push myself through it, wishing I could disappear.

"Paige, calm down. Tell me what happened. How all of this happened." He made a sweeping gesture with a shaking hand.

I forced myself to take one deep breath, and then another. If anyone would believe me, Sanjay would. He loved me.

"It was the park bench. The one I always sit on. I cut my hand, this one." I looked down at the offending limb. "And it made me sick. I passed out here, on the floor, and when I woke up, I was covered in this."

I held my arm out, stretched it out so he could see the

extent of it, all the while wondering how much farther it had spread beneath my clothes.

"I called them, I wanted help. I thought they could help me, but when they touched me. When they came in contact with the stuff, the infection, they…they died. You can see it with your own eyes. Their skin – like acid and —"

It was no use. I was crying. Sobbing so hard I was choking. He took a step towards me and I reeled back against the front door.

"No! Not any closer!" I cried out, sinking to the floor.

"Paige." He stepped out into the hall. "There's nothing on your arm. There's no infection. You know that, right?"

I tucked myself into the corner next to the door, feeling more and more of those cursed abscesses pop and leak their poison all over my skin. The poison that – somehow – did not turn my skin into soup like it did everyone else.

"It's all over me, Sanjay, it's everywhere!"

I held my arm in front of my face. The green, purple, and yellow were deeper, darker. It blazed within my skin like a sickly storm, ready to let loose a rain of toxic pus.

"Paige, let me help you. Please."

I looked up and saw, to my horror, that he had come closer, that he was reaching out to me.

"No! Get away from me!" I cried, recoiling as much as I could.

"Babe, listen to me. You're just having a panic attack, okay? There is nothing on your arm. Nothing. Now let me help you!"

"Get out! I hate you! I hate you, Sanjay, I hate you! I never want to see you again! Get out! GET OUT!" I screamed, every lie breaking my heart as I saw the pain it caused him.

Still, it had the effect I wanted and he backed up, his hands held up as if in surrender.

"I can't leave, Paige. There are two dead bodies in the kitchen. We have to call the police."

I knew he wouldn't leave. He wouldn't leave when he thought he could fix things. He never listened to me. He always thought he knew best and, in this case, it would get him killed if I didn't do something. I stood so suddenly that he flinched back.

He's afraid of you, my mind cried out mournfully, he thinks you did it.

I turned, yanking the front door open with my good hand and ran out of the house, slamming the door behind me. I was in my car by the time he made it to the front yard. I squealed out of the driveway, steering with just one hand, and sped off.

The car was quiet except for the sound of my heavy breathing, of the humming tires on the road, of the rushing wind. I'd left my phone back home. My shoulders slumped with the weight of the day. I found my way from the streets onto the highway. The road stretched onward forever into the night, lit only occasionally by pale buttery streetlights. The moon hung as swollen as that pregnant woman's belly in the black sky void of stars.

I switched hands on the steering wheel, using my left to scratch at a slight tingling on my left cheek. I felt a few of those damned bumps, still hard and small, only just gestating. Still I felt fine. Felt as healthy as ever. Felt perfect.

I would be fine. Everything could be fine. As long as I kept away from people, away from everyone. Sanjay was safe and I could keep others safe. I felt like I'd been preparing for something like this my whole life.

I took a moment to turn the radio on, filling the car with noise.

Now, scratching my neck and popping some of the riper abscesses, I drove on.

That Which The Ocean Gives and Takes Away

Newfoundland wasn't a stranger to the whimsical nature of the sea. The inhabitants of the island province had grown accustomed to the ocean's fickle nature, giving and taking in turn. But on the morning of August 3rd, the ocean gave back something strange indeed. The day before had been normal, no storm or wind gales, no disturbances of any kind. Yet, when dawn splashed across the horizon, the residents of the small community of Saint Mary's found a shipwreck on the gray expanse of Saint La Haye Beach.

It was a rusted husk, hung with ropes of seaweed and studded with thousands of large barnacles and cold-water coral patches. Its hull had sliced through the beach and the hulking metal behemoth canted to its starboard side, as the waves pounded its port side. It had been identified by the partial lettering on its hull as the *HMS Drake*, a frigate which had sunk in the 1920s.

The shipwreck, like the ocean that had brought it back, also took what it wanted. Since it arrived in Saint Mary's, teams of experts – police, scientists, doctors – had gone inside but only a few ever returned. When they did, the survivors babbled about voices and living things inside the hull. When asked about the missing members of their teams, they could give no real answers. Only that they had chosen to stay behind.

After that, the Canadian government tried to maintain a quarantine around the frigate. Any attempts to move it were futile, nothing seemed strong enough to pull it from its place in the sand. And despite their best efforts, civilians managed to sneak past the barricades to satisfy their morbid curiosity about the "haunted" ship.

More went missing than ever came back out again.

Two months later, the *Drake* had claimed over forty lives. Officials decided that one more team would be sent in to try and discover any survivors and to plant explosives. If the ship couldn't be moved then it would be destroyed.

The final team – appropriately named the Omega Team – consisted of four soldiers, an American representative from the CDC, a biologist, and a virologist.

Jean was that virologist. She was a Newfoundland native, though she had lived in Ottawa for the last three decades. She had accepted this mission, not as an excuse to visit her remaining family, but as an escape. Only grief and painful memories waited for her back home.

Newfoundland, much like the ocean that surrounded it,

was always ready to accept what was once its own. While her parents had passed years before, her extended family of aunts, uncles, and cousins were waiting. She had no doubt that they heard what had happened. It had made the news, her face and his had been put on the cover of every newspaper for a week after it happened. But her family wasn't the type to ask, wasn't the type to rock the boat with unpleasant topics. Instead, every aunt sought to fill the void that grief always leaves with food, lots and lots of food, too much food. The uncles talked only of fishing, of the weather, of the *Drake*.

It didn't erase her pain but it helped smooth the edges. Jean was glad that they allowed her to be silent, to rest, to think of nothing for the three days she stayed with them in Saint John's before she was required to meet the rest of the team in Saint Mary's.

Now Jean stood on the beach with the others, strangers to her, and stared up at the gray and green-spackled hull of the *Drake*. She wondered for the first time if this wasn't some passive suicide attempt. Enter the haunted ship and let fate decide.

The soldiers were talking but she couldn't seem to concentrate on what they were saying, couldn't even recall their names.

The *Drake* was haggard. The sea had eaten holes away in the hull, letting in the pathetic drizzle that fell from steel skies.

Each member was outfitted in a hazmat suit. Jean had the notion that the disappearances and strange accounts from survivors could be caused by some kind of deep-sea virus that the human body had no defense for.

Now, standing there on that beach, Jean felt a cold, thrill of fear. It was too late to back out now, or at least, Jean's pride wouldn't allow her to, so she followed the others as they made their way down the beach to where the frigate sat, sunk in the sand.

A fluorescent orange rope ladder was hanging from one of the larger holes in the hull. Jean tried to remember the blueprints she'd been sent but nothing came to mind. One by one, the team ascended and entered the *Drake*. The soldiers had heavy packs, in which sat the explosives that were to be set throughout the ship in order to guarantee its second death. Jean carried a small messenger bag which held every-thing she needed to take whatever samples she deemed were necessary.

Jean was the last one up the ladder. The wind picked up and the rope ladder fluttered out beneath her, clattering against the hull. She was grateful to reach the top where a soldier waited with a lowered hand to help her aboard. Inside, the ship was dark but for the dim light falling through the various holes in the hull and the bright lights from the flashlights each team member carried.

Jean suffered a strong wave of vertigo as she tried to adjust to the tilt of the floor and the walls that pressed in on them all. Ropes of algae and seaweed garlands decorated the hall. It was the veins that captured everyone's attention. The interior hull, the stairs, the walls were all covered in pale, fleshy veins that glowed with some interior phosphor-escence.

The soldiers were unnerved, though they tried to hide it. It was obvious in their stiffened stances and the way they clutched their guns. None of the reports had mentioned the veins. Jean knelt by the one closest to her and laid a hand on it. It was warm. Pleasantly so. She could feel it through her suit even. It also seemed to hum beneath her palm. She thought of taking a sample but the mental image of dragging a scalpel across the surface made her feel bad... like a criminal.

So, instead, she stood. She thought she could hear the humming in her head. The others were talking but it sounded like their voices were diluted, as though underwater. Jean looked around. They had entered the ship where the crew's quarters were housed. All the doors to the cabins were open, inviting. Jean watched the others as they spread out and each entered a room. It was not natural but it also seemed so normal.

Jean looked down the hall and, through the hanging debris, a door caught her eye. As she stared it seemed to be pulling her in. She took a step before realizing it.

A scream rent through the thick air and a soldier raced past her. He flung himself through the hole and out of the ship to the cold beach below. Jean gripped the jagged edges of the hull and peered down. Crimson sands and a body marked where he had landed and lay still.

A part of her told her to go back down the ladder. To escape.

Instead, Jean turned. None of the others had stepped out of the rooms they had entered. She could have gone to see what they were doing but a primal part of her understood that it would be sacrilegious to do so. Whatever was happening was beyond her control, beyond any of their controls.

So, she obeyed and went to the room that was meant for her.

Inside, Jean found a stranger. The room was small and contained only a soggy cot. The walls and floor were thick with veins and these ran across the man's body, puncturing his skin, diving deep inside.

Instantly, Jean felt a clear rush of revulsion. Whatever was infesting this ship was a virus, a parasite. The veins throbbed, the man stirred a bit, and she saw his lips curl into a smile.

He was alive.

It was feeding on him.

She turned, she meant to scream, meant to run.

Wait.

Jean waited, she turned back. One vein had detached from the wall and wavered in the air like a rattlesnake dancing to the song of a snake charmer's flute.

"What are you?"

If Jean should have felt strange speaking to a swaying tendril of flesh, she didn't. She felt numb and alert at the same time but, most of all, did not feel in danger at all.

A hermit crab finding a suitable shell and crawling inside. The glistening flank of a giant squid. Alien, strange stars. The crushing depths of the sea. A shadowed hulk at the bottom – the Drake. *The heavy weight of alien intelligence. A desire, a hunger, a need.*

From another room down the hall, Jean heard weeping. It started off violent, passionate, then quelled, quieted, and ended in a sigh.

"You're eating him."

Around her the organism shivered. The appendage in front of her seemed to bow a bit.

The man enters, a local dressed in plaid and jeans. An offer made, hesitance, then he lays on the bed. The veins slide off the wall, wreath him in warmth. He sleeps. He smiles.

Around her the rotting ship was quiet. Jean could not hear the others, could not know whether they were still onboard or had gone the way of the soldier.

Feeling of hunger, desperation, a plea.

"They're going to destroy the ship. We brought bombs and when we fail to return, they'll send more… or just bomb you from above."

Jean didn't know why she was telling the thing all this information, she couldn't even know if it understood her.

Images of people lying in the rooms, all asleep and covered in the organism's flesh. Peace. Mutual survival.

"I won't. I don't know how you convinced them to lie down for you, but I won't."

An image of Jean lying down, at peace, happy. Massive albino limbs stretching out, great claws digging deep into the sand, pulling the shipwreck back out into the depths to rest once more.

Jean shook her head.

Hidden in the deep sea among the blind fish and chilled currents. A fleshy mass protruding: the head of the thing that lived within. Skin splits, opens: a mouth, a deafening call. A response from the stars. Salvation.

Jean felt tired, so tired. She left the room and went down the hall, checking for the others. She found them in their rooms. All had laid down for the being and its veins threaded with theirs. In the room with one of the soldiers, Jean thought about taking his bag and planting the explosives herself, then she shook her head and returned to the hole in the hull where the ladder hung.

Jean.

"Why should I? Why should I give myself to you?"

The feeling of their very first kiss on their very first date. Henry standing in his tuxedo at the alter. The sound of his laughter. Henry standing in their green kitchen, cooking eggs.

"Don't! Don't you dare!"

The pain was sharper than whatever atmospheric influence the creature managed to control. Jean stepped onto the edge, the toes of her boots hanging over, the waves pounding the sand beneath. The soldier, she saw, had managed to pull himself a few meters up the beach.

Jean going to the room and lying down. The organism's probing tongues pierce her skin. A moment of pain. Henry waiting for her with open arms. A second chance.

A second chance.

Her vision blurred. Without thinking she pulled the helmet from her head and wiped at her face. It didn't matter after all. There was no virus on the ship. The creature hadn't forced anyone to do anything. It had just offered something that was near impossible to refuse.

Henry laughing as he threw a snowball at her. Her teaching him how to ski. A warm night spent by the fireplace with big mugs of beer.

An offer of a second chance with no sad ending. No tears. No heartbreak. No murder by the hands of a cruel man high on drugs on the streets of Ottawa. An offer. An offer in exchange for her life to feed its survival.

She trembled on the edge. Jean tried to remember her life as it was. The entity helped her see it so clearly.

Pain. Working at a sterile lab, white on gray on white, underappreciated, unseen. Returning to an empty house. A void aching inside. A missing piece.

She looked over her shoulder where the open door still beckoned. She tried to imagine what life would be like, living in a coma until death, living a lie.

Henry waiting, arms open, warmth, a life without pain – guaranteed to be without pain. Manufactured, but perfect. False, but satisfactory.

She closed her eyes against the threatening tears. Was it weak to surrender? Jean turned and went back to her room, unzipping her hazmat suit as she did so. It was warm there. At first, she had assumed that lying on the floor would be uncomfortable, but the flesh of the organism that covered it was soft, warm, yielding. Its probes detached from the walls and hovered over her body waiting.

Jean closed her eyes and nodded.

The pain was brief. A fatigue like none other stole over her and Jean slipped away.

When she opened her eyes next, she forgot all about the *Drake*, the organism, the life she had left.

"Wakey wakey," Henry said, leaning over her on his elbow.

He touched the tip of her nose with a kiss as soft as butterfly wings. Jean smiled and wrapped her arms around his neck, bringing him down for a deeper embrace.

The soldier in the sand was noticed three hours after the Omega Team failed to return. He was in shock from various broken bones and blood loss from his fall, shrieking about an offer made by a tempting devil that sheathed the ship in its sour temptations. Authorities waited an additional two hours for the others, but no other survivors exited the *Drake* so the final order was given that the following day, the ship was to be bombed from above.

This plan was never executed for the next watery dawn saw the beach barren. The ocean had received back what it had given. The *Drake* was gone. And with it, all the missing souls aboard.

THE DROUGHT OF BURHAM

Repressing a yawn, I sat staring at my old scratched-up desk, which was covered in paperwork, a couple of plastic cacti, an old phone, and my father's standing clock.

It was only two in the afternoon and warm slants of sunlight streamed in through the blinds, illuminating the interior of the police station, and casting a warm yellow hue to the various posters on the walls and to the deer head mounted above the entrance. I was the only one in the station. Constable Nate Burns was doing a routine patrol and Chief Inspector Jude Monroe was likely out on the Windrash River as usual.

I reached out and picked up the desk phone, listening to see if it was still working. An abrasive buzz let me know that, yes, it did indeed still have a dial tone. Returning the receiver to its cradle, I pulled my cellphone from my pocket to check for notifications. Nothing.

Then the desk phone jangled, causing me to jump. My cell phone slipped from my fingers and clattered against the wooden floor. Heart pounding, I answered.

"Burham Police Department, how may I help you?"

"Nora, you still there?" the Chief Inspector asked with a loud chuckle. "Go on and close up. My knees swear it'll be a quiet night. I hear the Buckhead Pub'll be hosting some live music – Conrad's boy and his friends will be playing. You should go!"

I sighed. "Thanks, Chief."

"Ta."

I hung up and leaned back in my chair, stretching my hands above my head, feeling each vertebra crackling. In the silence of the afternoon, my clock ticking away the seconds in booms. I reached down, grabbed my cell, and slipped it back into my pocket. Standing, I made the rounds of the station, checking to make sure the coffee maker was off, that the windows were closed, and the answering machine set to redirect all calls to the Chief Inspector's cellphone. Finally, I went to the front door and yanked it free from its crooked frame. With a wretched squeal, the door opened, revealing a tall man dressed all in black with his fist raised.

We stood together, on either side of the threshold, trapped in a long and heavy pause. I cleared my throat.

"Afternoon. Can I help you, Mr...."

I knew everyone in little Burham of course, everyone who lived here knew one another.

"Amos Tannis." His voice was deep, tinted with an

accent of somewhere outside of Burham.

The last name also rang a distant bell.

"Tannis?" I said after he stood there, providing nothing more.

"Howard Tannis is my brother."

The bell chimed true with remembrance. Howard Tannis was a writer of some renown, who had moved here a few months back to get away from city interference, as he put it. 'Was' because we found him dead in a field a month ago.

"Ah. Mr. Tannis. Would you care to come in?"

"He's dead, isn't he? We usually text each other once a week. After a month of silence, I decided I needed to come down here."

I bit my lip, my guts churning. Normally the Chief took care of notifying next of kin. I'd never had to.

Until now. "I'm sorry, Mr. Tannis, but he did pass. Heart failure. He never talked about family, so we had no idea who to contact."

The man's face paled to a point that I worried he might just faint right then and there.

He caught his second wind, grabbing the doorframe and swaying a bit. "Dead?"

The Buckhead was a short walk from the police station so that's where I brought him. He sat across from me, head planted firmly in the palms of his hands, an untouched pint next to his right elbow. I was halfway through mine. The only music playing was soft acoustic country. It was too early for the band, they wouldn't be in for another few hours.

However, the Buckhead was as comfortable place as any while I waited for Mr. Tannis to regain his composure.

"You said it was heart failure?" his voice barely a whisper.

"Yes." I took a sip.

"There was an autopsy done?"

I paused. "No. The doctor here didn't think it was necessary."

At this, his head jerked up, his eyes glistening.

"So, you found my brother dead and didn't do an autopsy? Then you buried him without waiting to contact his family? How – how absurd!"

I opened my mouth, shut it, and opened it again. "He never told anyone about having family, sir, we –"

"I'm his family, Sergeant Cooke!"

"I'm really sorry, Mr. Tannis."

The man stared at me, his chest heaving, and his face reddened. I had the crazy thought that he might just have a heart attack and join his brother in the great beyond. Instead, he sat back again and looked away, biting at his thumb nail.

"Is there a hotel here? Some place I can rent a room?" His voice was still now, careful.

"Well, there is the Larkfield Priory Hotel, a bit swanky for my tastes, or George will rent you a simple room here, above the bar for cheap. I think he throws in breakfast too."

Mr. Tannis nodded and stood. I watched him fumble a small wallet out of his pocket and he tossed a bill onto the table, turned, and left without a word.

I waited a bit to finish my beer, then I gave George – the owner and acting bartender – a wave before heading out.

The next morning, the air above the fields was hazy with uncharacteristic summer heat. Usually the early mornings were my favourite part of the day, clear and with a chilly bite to it. This summer had been dry and hot though, with no true relief even in the latest part of the night. Now the low sun was baking what dew the fields had managed to gather into a fine mist that drifted across the green acres that ran along the length of the road. The sky was a washed-out blue, clear of any cloud, promising for yet another blistering day.

My bike jangled over the cobblestone streets as I glided my way down the hill to the station for the start of my morning shift. I glanced down from time to time to the basket on the front of my handlebars to make sure my lunch hadn't managed to bounce out during my commute. While quaint, the cobblestone roads weren't conducive for bike riding.

I sped around a slight curve, ducking beneath the reaching branches of an old oak tree that leaned over the street. The road levelled out and I let myself slow to a stop, right in front of the station. I brought my bike around back, not bothering to lock it, and carried my lunch with me to the front of the station, unlocking the door. Nate was inside, sitting behind his own desk with his feet kicked up onto it, and hat resting over his face. He snored a little.

We always worked Saturday mornings together so I wasn't surprised to see a small white paper bag – slightly crumpled – waiting on my desk for me. I could smell the freshly baked croissant from here. His wife owned a small bakery in town. It was an unspoken deal we had. Nate was supposed to open the station at six in the morning but instead, he would arrive at six and sleep at his desk. Then I would open it at eight when I got in for my shift and not a word was mentioned to the Chief.

I tucked my lunch box into the small communal fridge in the tiny kitchenette at the back of the station and set the coffee maker going for when Nate woke up. While it bubbled and hissed, I made myself a cup of black tea and carried it back to my desk, mouth already watering at the thought of Mrs. Burns's homemade croissant.

The station door opened just as I was reaching inside, fingertips brushing against the buttery still-warm bread. Mr. Tannis slammed it behind him and, out of the corner of my eye, I saw Nate flinch.

"Mr. Tannis, good morning," I said, reluctantly pulling my hand out of the bag.

"The guy who rented me my room said the station opens at six!" he said, already red in the face and bristling.

I glanced over at Nate. I couldn't be sure, but I thought I saw a smile beneath his hat.

"I knocked *and* called!" Mr. Tannis finished, fists clenching, looming over my desk in a wholly uncomfortable manner.

I stood.

"What can I help you with today, Mr. Tannis? How was your room at the Buckhead?"

"Is that the Chief?" He nodded at Nate.

"No, that is Constable Burns."

"And does Constable Burns always sleep on the job?"

"Only when Constable Burns has spent a rowdy night with the missus, sir."

Nate's shoulders shook as he tried to contain his laughter while still pretending to be asleep, Mr. Tannis was less amused.

"I am assuming you have my brother's address on file?" he said through gritted teeth.

"I am sure we do. Shall I look it up for you?"

I felt a little bad for having such fun getting his back up, so I tried to rein it in. Sitting again, I turned on my computer. Every second it took to boot up felt like days with Mr. Tannis looming over me.

"Here we are. Mr. Howard Tannis. He had been renting Graystone Cottage, on the edge of Blackheath farm."

"And what about his possessions, don't tell me you've thrown them in the bin."

"Well, I wouldn't rightly know, Mr. Tannis. You could ask Eira MacGowan. She was the one renting it to him, likely she's put it all in storage." I eyed the bakery bag.

"Fine. Let's go then," he said.

"Sorry?"

"Take me to this MacGowan woman. I think that much is owed to me considering."

I glanced over at Nate, still pretending to be asleep. I sighed. I stood.

Eira was out in her garden when I pulled up her winding dirt road. Despite being a talented green thumb, even her plants were wilting under the dry and relentless summer sun. Her farm was modest but well kept, with a few snuffling pigs, haughty chickens, and naughty goats roaming around. Her garden was large and its contents usually won her a gold medal or two in the town's annual competition. She lived alone in a small farmhouse made of gray stone and dominated by the huge chimney on one side.

Eira stood from where she'd been kneeling between her tomato plants when she heard the car tires crunch over the dirt. She was wearing a simple gray dress and a sunhat bleached an off-white by long days spent in the sun.

I got out of the patrol car and lifted a hand in greeting, which she returned in her usual serene manner, a half smile twisting the left side of her mouth. Mr. Tannis strode towards her and I jogged to catch up.

"You must be Eira MacGowan?" His voice was loud, an affront to Eira's quiet garden.

"Nora, how nice of you to come by. If I had known, I would have put a pot on," Eira said.

She was maintaining her smile, but her eyes narrowed as Mr. Tannis barged through her garden. I stepped over the tomato he'd stomped on. Eira was very proud of her garden and with that pride came a vengeful possessiveness.

At being snubbed, Mr. Tannis took another step towards Eira. He was taller than her, but she didn't flinch or back up. I cleared my throat.

"Morning Eira. Hope you don't mind our intrusion. This is Mr. Tannis. He's Howard's brother."

"Ah, I see," she replied, her voice cool as she eyed his path of destruction through her carefully maintained rows of carrots, peas, potatoes, and herbs.

"I've come for Howard's effects," Mr. Tannis said, louder than necessary.

Eira finally looked up him, her movements as languid as a cat who knows it's on its own territory.

"Of course. Follow me."

She turned and slipped through her plants as gently as though she were a simple breeze. I followed Mr. Tannis and cringed every time he put his foot down. Eira led us past her small house and into the field beyond it. Here dogrose, cornflower, and ragged robins added their subtle fragrances to the dry, dusty scent of the thick grasses which rose in an itchy haze around my face. Eira followed a well-worn walking path through the field, which led the three of us to the small stone cottage hidden just around a copse of trees.

It was a single story, constructed of the same gray stones as Eira's farmhouse. It had a smaller chimney and two windows which framed the heavy wooden front door. A small bench sat under a large oak tree, which grew to the left of the cottage. I could see a metal bucket full of sand and cigarettes next to it.

Eira approached the door and pushed it open, entering as she did. Mr. Tannis followed at a pace that seemed to imply that he thought Eira might steal something if he wasn't there to watch her. Before I joined them, I looked back the way we had come, closed my eyes, and took a deep breath, savouring the taste of grass, flowers, and summer.

It was dim and cool inside. Eira stood by the small fireplace, pointedly ignoring the prowling Mr. Tannis as he opened drawers and cupboards. The cottage was composed of three rooms: a large common room with the fireplace, an overstuffed loveseat, desk and matching chair, and a kitchen area with a tiny stove, sink, mini fridge, and radio. Two doors stood side by side across the room from the front door. These were open. One led to a bathroom with a cramped clawfoot tub and the other led to a bedroom dominated by a lumpy bed, which had been stripped of sheets.

"Where are his things, Miss MacGowan? There's nothing here!" Mr. Tannis stopped going through the cupboards and stomped back to the middle of the common room with fists planted firmly on his hips.

"His things, Mr. Tannis?"

"His stuff. His belongings. His possessions, Miss MacGowan!"

Eira walked past him to where the old desk stood beneath one of the front windows and picked up the laptop that lay closed on it. She held it out towards Mr. Tannis.

"This is his. His clothes I boxed up. They are in the bedroom next to the bed."

He snatched the computer.

"That's it? You're telling me my brother moved here with only his laptop and his clothes?" His voice was rising, rage simmering beneath a carefully controlled exterior.

"There was his camera. The police have that. It was found on his body," Eira said.

"That's correct. We have that at the station and can return it to you there," I offered, hoping to end this awkward scene as soon as possible.

"Did you find him? She said that he was found on the edge of your property," Mr. Tannis said.

"I did. Just beyond that copse of oaks we passed. He

51

must have been out there all night for there was dew on his face and his skin was chilled," Eira replied.

"Heart failure doesn't run in my family."

"It was a tragedy for sure, Mr. Tannis. Let's head back to the station and we can get you your brother's camera." I stepped through the front door and back into the sunlight.

Mr. Tannis looked back and forth from Eira to me and back again. He finally settled on her.

"I'll be back. I want to see where you found him," he said.

"I'm sorry for your loss, Mr. Tannis. Your brother was a kind man," Eira replied.

Back at the station, Chief Inspector Monroe was lounging in his chair, eating a croissant, while the paper bag on my desk was mysteriously empty. He stood after brushing crumbs from the front of his uniform and held out a hand to Mr. Tannis.

"You must be Howard Tannis's brother. My condolences."

"Sergeant Cooke told me that you didn't have my brother autopsied. Why is that?"

"Why don't you take a seat, Mr. Tannis." The Chief kept smiling until Mr. Tannis finally sat, then continued. "Now, when your brother was found, he didn't have a mark on him to indicate that there may have been foul play involved or that he had committed suicide."

"Maybe you didn't know Howard but I did. He never smoked a day in his life, he exercised, and was as healthy as a horse. There's no way he died of heart failure at thirty-five, especially with no family history of it!"

I thought of the bucket of sand and cigarettes by the cottage but said nothing. Instead, I slipped back to my desk and sat down, sipping at my now cold cup of tea, listening as I did.

"That may as well be, but things like this can happen you know," the Chief said.

There was a squeal as a chair scraped against the floor.

"No, they don't. Where is his body? I want to see him."

"Well, we tried to find any information on his family but couldn't. Your brother didn't tell us much in the short time he was here, and we didn't know the password to his laptop –"

"Where is he?" Mr. Tannis demanded.

"We buried him. A right Catholic funeral. The whole town turned out, you know, all very respectful and that."

I thought back to the funeral. It had been respectful. Howard Tannis was a stranger but that didn't mean we didn't want him resting in peace. Mrs. Vera Langsdale had even created a beautiful wreath of lilies for the very occasion.

The silence behind my back weighed heavier with every second that passed. Then there was a rush of wind as Mr. Tannis stormed past me and left the station, making the whole building shudder with how he slammed the door. I felt more than heard the Chief come up behind me. He reached over and placed a camera on my desk.

"Mind delivering this to our visitor?" he asked.

I sighed and finished off my tea.

I found Mr. Tannis back at the Buckhead eating an early lunch at the bar. George was polishing glasses in front of him, talking on as he did.

"My great-grandfather said it was quite the terrifying sight, seeing those two tearing through the streets all ablaze with St. Elmo's fire," George said.

"Entertaining our guest, George?" I called out as I entered.

Mr. Tannis looked up from his sandwich and frowned slightly. I pulled the camera from my bag and placed it carefully on the bar next to his plate.

"Just educating Mr. Tannis on the local history, Nora."

"He's telling me a ghost story," Mr. Tannis scoffed.

George, a proud and practiced storyteller, looked hurt.

"Ghost stories are a part of a town's history, Mr. Tannis. Fact of the matter is, you'll hear it nowhere better than George." I smiled at the elderly bartender as he puffed up with pride.

"I didn't see any ghostly judge in the streets last night, him or his lady wife," Mr. Tannis grumbled.

"Ah see, the priest led all the folk of Burham in a town-wide exorcism. That judge was a nasty one, but his wife was worse. Carol Humphrey, she's the great grand-daughter of Mary Humphrey who acted as a midwife you know, she said Mary attended three of the judge's wife's births. But they never had no children, you understand? Those babes never saw their own first birthdays, may God rest their tiny souls. Well, the Lady Tanfield wouldn't be so easily put away like her husband.

"It was a long night, it was. The whole town stayed up chanting their psalms and the priest was in town square with his bible, his candle, and his blessed bell. Finally, just as the faint pink light of dawn was peeking up, it worked, and the nasty Lady Tanfield was sealed away in a bottle.

The priest took it and threw it into the Windrash, you know. Those waters are pure and fresh and keep that wretched spirit trapped. But her anger only grows each year, and she waits for the river to dry up so she can escape."

"The river at the edge of town?" was Mr. Tannis's only response.

"That's the one," George said.

"You call that a river with how low it is? It's barely more than a creek." Mr. Tannis shoved his plate from him. "Put that on my room tab, will you?"

George frowned as the other man stood. The bartender looked at me and I gave a slight shrug.

"I'm going back to Blackheath farm. I want to see where my brother was found. You can drive me, that will give me a moment to look through the photos on this camera," Mr. Tannis said, walking past me.

I bristled at his tone but followed anyway. The Chief had told me to look after our guest after all. Sitting next to me in my patrol car, Mr. Tannis scrolled through his brother's photos. I knew he wouldn't find anything. We'd gone through it ourselves when we'd found it. Mr. Tannis would find nothing more than photos of the native flowers, town buildings, and the Windrash.

"Howard told me he was coming down here to write a book. He said he knew this town would inspire him." Mr. Tannis's voice was low, mournful.

"He did mention that," I said, wishing the drive to Eira's farm wasn't so long.

"Why would he think that? This place is tiny and has nothing of interest in it."

"That just means you haven't tried Mrs. Burns's blueberry scones." I forced a laugh and got silence in return.

I glanced over and saw that he'd reached the last photo in the camera's memory: one of Eira standing in her garden with a wide grin, her dress billowing out in a bit of wind. Mr. Tannis's face was screwed up in a tight frown.

Eira came out of her farmhouse when she heard the car roll up, hands dusted with flour. Mr. Tannis put the strap of the camera around his neck and got out to meet her.

"Afternoon. I didn't expect you out for another visit so soon," she said.

"The cops aren't being very helpful, so I figured I'd come back."

"And you want to see where I found him?"

Mr. Tannis nodded and the three of us, led by Eira, went back through the field of grass behind the farmhouse.

"Miss MacGowan, do you know what Howard was working on out here?"

In that moment, surrounded by the haze of heat and pollen, and his voice shaking with emotion, I felt bad for the surly man. Eira didn't look back as she led us past the copse of trees and the small cottage.

"A book, I believe," she said.

"I know that!" Mr. Tannis shouted.

Eira and I stopped in unison. She finally turned, but when she did, she looked at me, not at him.

"I accessed his computer and found nothing! Now why wouldn't there be a copy, a backup, any trace of this so-called book?" he continued.

"It's like the Chief said, Mr. Tannis, we didn't have his

password. And because he died of natural causes, we didn't bother to take it in to the station. Maybe he just hadn't had started it yet," I said.

Eira turned away again and continued through the grass. After a moment, Mr. Tannis followed. Ahead something stood, bleary in the heat, becoming clearer with every step. It was a group of old gray stones, arranged in a circle. Many were weathered down to waist height, but a few still stood six feet tall, casting vivid shadows over the ground. Eira stopped in the middle of the ring. She pointed just beyond the tallest stone.

"I found him there, Mr. Tannis. Just beyond the stone ring. Lying on his back, his eyes open, staring up into the morning sky. And around his neck was that very camera." Eira nodded toward where the mentioned device rested against Mr. Tannis's chest.

Mr. Tannis stepped into the ring, staring up at the stones. They were etched with deep sigils, coloured with lichen. The middle of the ring was bare, in fact nothing grew inside the ring at all.

"Why would he have been here in the middle of the night?" he asked, quietly, as if to himself.

"Perhaps he wished to catch a stunning tableau of the stones in the moonlight. That night was a full moon if I remember, correctly. As tonight will be," Eira said.

She placed a palm against the stone closest to her.

"Howard had a deep interest in this place. He believed it to be the site of ceremony for some pagan tribe he claimed to have lived here before Burham was a town."

"Eira," I protested. "I think Mr. Tannis has had enough

of folklore for today."

"Paganism? Like witches?" Mr. Tannis turned to look at Eira.

"I suppose something similar to that effect," Eira said, looking over her shoulder at him with a smile. "They believed this ring of stones had power, that they could receive answers for their prayers here, that something could protect them should they ask it to. That's why they marked the stones with these runes."

"Of course, Howard mentioned in an email that he wanted to do a horror novel for a change! He must have come here to do research on the pagan history. I'm sure your locals were excellent sources of information considering how that old man behind the bar went on and on about that ghost story for the entirety of lunch," Mr. Tannis uttered a cold laugh.

I decided I wasn't much a fan of him in that moment. George was well meaning and did a lot for the community, volunteering for festivals and putting on special events for the town.

"That explains why he rented out that dismal cottage, to be close to the stone ring," Mr. Tannis looked at Eira intensely. "There was a picture of you on his camera. You two must have spent a lot of time together."

Eira ignored his tone and began to walk back the way we'd come. "He came over once and a while to ask me questions."

"What are you? The town historian?" He laughed.

The sun was directly above us now and the miasma of scents baking off the field had become stifling.

"Not a historian by any right. Just someone who knows things," came Eira's reply, floating with the floral seedlings on the low breeze.

We went back to her farmhouse and she invited us in, turning on her gas stove to heat some water. Her home was similar to the layout of the stone cottage, except on a larger scale. The long common room was dominated on the right-hand wall by a six-foot-wide fireplace, and two faded couches and a rocking chair framing a handwoven rug stood in front of the hearth. Beyond that was a wooden table and four chairs. The left-hand third of the open space was the kitchen decorated with hanging bundles of flowers, plants, and herbs drying for use later. A small staircase led to a loft above the fireplace where Eira's bedroom was, you could see the wide bed and multitude of houseplants from the front door. A small door next to the kitchen led to the tiny bathroom.

The whole place was heavy with the smell of baking bread. I went to the cupboard above the sink and pulled down three mugs and placed them on the scarred kitchen table. A small jar sat in the middle, I unscrewed its metal lid, and plucked out three teabags, dropping one into each mug.

Mr. Tannis sat, looking uncomfortable, clasping his hands before him on the table. I stood at the opposite end of the table and Eira waited in the kitchen. The three of us stayed like this, frozen in limbo, until the kettle whistled. Then the world fell into motion again. I moved to the fridge to grab the glass milk container and Eira poured water into each mug. We sat.

"Your brother was an extremely kind man," Eira said. "It broke my heart to find him like that. And yes, we spent many evenings together and he asked me many things about the ring of stones, about the village, about the river. I'm sure it is as you said, that he was working on a horror novel of some kind but he never shared anything with me. Not a single outline or page of his draft."

"Sugar?" I asked, pushing a small jar towards Mr. Tannis.

"No," he said. "I take it black."

He was distracted. The whole table positively shook with the way he bounced his knee underneath it. Suddenly, Mr. Tannis stood with a jerk, causing tea to slosh over the rims of all three mugs. He paced along the wall towards the fireplace. There, he fiddled with the small stones, the picture frames, the braided sage, and every little knickknack Eira had on the mantle.

"Miss MacGowan, be frank with me," he said, his back to us. "You found him after all and I want to believe you two had become …friends at least, while he was here. Do you think he died of heart failure like everyone is telling me? Despite being completely healthy, despite being young, despite there being no family history?"

Eira looked across the table at me and I watched her, waiting to see what she would say.

"Yes, Mr. Tannis. I believe his heart gave out. I believe it gave out due to fear."

My shoulders slumped and I sighed. I leaned back in the chair and sipped at my tea.

"Fear?"

From across the room, I could hear the incredulity in his voice and see how his shoulders stiffened.

"You said George told you a story, a town ghost story," Eira began.

He barked out a harsh laugh and spun, the last item he'd picked up still in his hand: a handmade picture frame decorated with seashells.

"What? You think my brother was scared to death of some ghost story?" He stormed up to the table, grabbing Eira by her upper arm.

"Mr. Tannis!" I shouted and stood so fast I spilled tea over my hand.

I cursed and put the mug down, shaking my fingers and trying to get the hot liquid off.

"You should run cold water over it," Eira said, unbothered by Mr. Tannis's brutish behaviour.

She stood and looked down at his hand. He looked down too, seemed to realize what he was doing, and stepped back with a sheepish look.

"Whatever you may believe, Mr. Tannis, I know what I saw on your brother's face: a look of pure terror," she said. "I warned him not to go out in the fields at night. The river Windrash runs along the back of the field and we've had no rain for weeks, the river is running low – dangerously low."

"You're insane." Mr. Tannis was shouting, spittle flying across the surface of the table. "You and that batty old man at the bar, this whole fucking town probably. You think a dead woman got my brother? More likely you killed him and the entire town is in on it!"

He didn't wait for either of us to say anything, just stormed out of the house. I had the car keys though so I knew he wouldn't get far.

"Make sure you put some salve on that when you get back to the station," Eira said.

"I don't know if you should've told him that about his brother," I replied gently.

She shrugged and smiled. Knowing there was nothing more to be said, I went outside. I was right, he hadn't gotten far. He leaned against the passenger side door, his face stormy. We didn't speak the entire way back to town.

"Full moon tonight."

I jerked out of my comfortable doze, yanking my feet off my desk in the station. Nate nudged my shoulder playfully and then sat on the edge of my desk.

"You going to the Buckhead tonight?" he asked. "It's trivia night."

"Not tonight, I have some stuff I need to do," I said through my yawn.

"You sure? Our team has room for one more. I heard George is giving the winners their drinks free."

"Maybe if I get done early, I'll swing round," I said.

My desk phone rang.

"Maybe see you later then, Nora. Don't get into too much trouble out there," Nate said, waving goodbye as he left the station for the night.

"Burham Police Station, how can I help you?" I said into the phone.

"Nora, that you?"

"George? What can I do you for?"

"That fellow of yours, he's here right now and more than a little toshed. Now, I'll admit, some of that is my fault, but he's a bit upset you know, and stirring up some of my regulars."

I sighed and looked around the station. I was the only one left. Again.

"I'll be right over, George."

Mr. Tannis stood in the middle of the bar, an empty pint glass in one hand and the other pointing at Samuel Marsh, the middle school principal.

"Maybe if you were teaching kids right, you wouldn't have such batty citizens!" he shouted.

Samuel's round face and bald head were beet-red, his fists were raised, and it looked like he was a second away from smashing Mr. Tannis in the face.

"Now, now, I see George has been serving his famous full moon beer. Why else would grown men be acting like boys?" I called out.

Samuel looked at me and dropped his fists. Mr. Tannis turned slowly, made eye contact, and slammed his glass to the counter.

"Well, well, well. If it isn't Constable Good-for-Nothing," he said.

"Don't tell me you forgot about our dinner plans, Mr. Tannis," I replied.

He paused. His face screwed up as his brain struggled to function under the haze of alcohol.

"Dinner?" he slurred finally.

I sidled up to him and slipped my arm through his.

"You said you'd let me take you out to the best place in town. My treat of course."

He swayed against me. I took a tentative step forward and he followed my lead. Relieved, I led him out of the Buckhead and to the patrol car.

"You're taking me in *that*?" he said.

"I don't have a car, remember? Now come on, dinner won't eat itself."

Kelly Rose led us to a table in the back of Rose's Nook, right by the kitchen entrance and away from the other patrons. She placed two glasses of water down and gave me a wink. Her husband leaned out from the kitchen.

"Nora, love! Two chef specials?" he said with a grin.

"That'd be perfect, Isaac," I said.

"I'm – I'm sorry, Nora was it?"

I looked across the table at Mr. Tannis.

"I'm not usually like this." His voice was barely above a whisper. "I – when I found out about Howard, I guess a bit of my heart broke off. I knew something was wrong, you know. I could feel it."

I was shocked and a little horrified to see tears brimming in his eyes.

"Mr. Tannis, it's fine, really." I forced myself to reach out and put a hand over one of his.

He clutched at my hand like it was a lifeline and he'd been drowning. I tried not to pull away.

"We were twins, you see. Fraternal. He was my brother and my best friend," Mr. Tannis continued. "He was more talented than me though. Leagues of talent. You could tell just by his writing. I always envied him for all the things he excelled at."

The man's bottom lip trembled as he stared at my hand engulfed in his. My skin itched at the sweat on his palms so I was grateful when Kelly showed up with two plates. It gave me an excuse to pull my hand away and wipe it discreetly on the cloth napkin in my lap.

"Here you go. Two chef specials, enjoy!"

She set the plates down carefully, revealing rabbit stew served on creamy mashed potatoes. Mr. Tannis stared down at his plate, hands limp on either side.

"Do you believe in ghosts, Nora?" he asked, his voice still clogged from unshed tears.

"You should eat, Mr. Tannis. The food will help."

He took a bite, another, and then another. Through his fourth mouthful, he asked; "Do you believe a ghost killed my brother?"

The full moon had risen above the horizon and its bony face cast a pale veil of light over the fields. This far from town, the stars shone unimpeded by light pollution, and the black sky stretched up, and up, and up forever. There were no streetlights out here. It felt like blasphemy to have any kind of artificial light and, since I was as familiar with these country roads as with the back of my hand, I drove with my headlights off, only the moon guiding my way.

"This – this izznt way to Buckhead," Mr. Tannis slurred.

I ignored him. The windows of my car were rolled down. It had cooled off a tad, but not much. I turned right onto the dirt road that led to Eira's farm, driving slowly over the rocks and dips. I heard the scrape of glass on glass.

"Oops, broke id," he mumbled.

I glanced over to see Mr. Tannis reaching down between his legs. He pulled up the seashell picture frame he'd taken from Eira's farmhouse and then left in the patrol car. The glass front was completely shattered.

"Wait," he said.

As Eira's farmhouse came into view, I could see that all the windows were dark. There was not a light to be seen.

"Izzt – Izzt id you?" Mr. Tannis's words were nearly unintelligible.

I didn't look over. I knew what picture was in that frame, because I had made the frame myself when I was sixteen for my best friend, who also happened to be my cousin. I knew I was in that picture, as was Eira.

Eira's mother had taken it of us as we stood in the middle of the stone ring, wearing flower crowns and nothing else. I heard a thump as Mr. Tannis's head hit the dash. He moaned. I looked over nervously. He was slumped over, passed out.

I let out the breath I'd been holding. Kelly Rose's daughter, Beatrice, worked at the local pharmacy but I'd been worried she might have gotten the dose wrong since we hadn't known Mr. Tannis's exact weight. But he was sleeping as soundly as a baby.

Eira waited for us in front of the farm. Once parked, I joined her on the passenger side of my patrol car.

"We'll need to hurry. The night is getting late. And dark," she said.

I opened the door, pulling Mr. Tannis from the seat and onto the dirt drive. He was heavier than he looked, maybe that was why it had taken so long for the drugs to kick in. Looking down at him, I felt a pang of guilt – in the cold jab at the back of my neck, in the itchy sweat that slid down my spine. Eira reached into the car and pulled out the picture frame.

"He must have stepped on it when he was getting into the car," I said.

She laid it on the hood of the car, its remaining glass bits glinting like silver teeth in the moonlight.

"Let's go, dearest Nora. You can feel it, right?"

I could. It was a sourness in the air that you could only taste at the back of your throat, it was a dry, prickling cold that slunk about beneath the unnatural heat. I nodded and we bent down together and each grabbed one of Mr. Tannis's arms. He was heavy but we were strong and, together, we carried him through the field of grass, past the copse of trees, the stone cottage, and to the stone circle.

She dropped his arm as soon as we were inside the ring, leaving me slumped with his weight. I couldn't bring myself to drop him too, instead I laid him down as gently as I could.

I arranged him so he was on his back with his head pointing to the east. Eira put a small stone knife on the ground above his head and a second below his feet.

Eira held her hand out to me. I took the lavender crown from her and pulled it tenderly onto Mr. Tannis's head. Compared to the bright violet flowers, his face looked bleached in the light of the full moon. Plucking two blossoms, I put one on each of his eyes. His eyelashes looked damp, as though still wet from his tears at dinner.

A lump grew in my throat and I stood quickly, looking away. I swallowed back the guilt and doubt, I tried not to think about Mr. Tannis crying about his brother.

Eira stood at the northern point of the ring, in front of the tallest stone. I stood in front of the shortest one, in the southern point. She smiled at me and I forced myself to smile back. Then we undressed and tossed our clothes off to the side, out of the circle. Her hair was unbound, a dark cascade over her shoulders and I reached up, pulling off my hair elastic, allowing my blond hair to frame me in the same way. The moonlight draped us in silver and ivory.

Behind Eira, farther to the north where the Windrash River wound its path, a haze of Elmo's fire rose. The river was the shallowest there, it was there that Lady Tanfield would be manifesting. It was there that she had been manifesting every night for the last three months when the river had reached its lowest since her exorcism. In all that time, we'd been careful. We'd put up stone wards and lavender wreaths along the property line of Blackheath farm, hoping to contain her here and here alone – but every full moon, she had grown stronger and travelled farther and farther from the river.

"We have no other choice," Eira said, startling me out of my thoughts. "Would you rather it be one of our own?"

I shook my head, not trusting myself to speak. A faint shriek rose from the direction of the river. There wasn't much time before Lady Tanfield would find us as she had Howard Tannis three months ago. Eira and I stepped toward the middle of the ring. Mr. Tannis hadn't moved in all this time. He was sleeping peacefully. I found consolation in that. I doubted he would feel a thing.

We knelt together in silence. This was not like the rituals we performed during the solstices, full of cheerful chanting and song. This ceremony was older, darker, and meant for the spaces between sounds. We unbuttoned his shirt and laid his chest bare. Eira picked up the knife by Mr. Tannis's head. I picked up the one by his feet. Our eyes met over his body. This time she did not smile.

Another wail rode the nocturnal breeze to the stone ring, closer this time, and fiercer. The stone knives did not shine in the moonlight as we held them above our heads, instead they drank it all into themselves and flashed like lightning as they plunged downward.

Eira's found its mark just at the base of his throat and mine found it just above his groin. The feeling of the stone knife slicing through skin and muscle was unnervingly familiar despite my only having done this same ritual once before.

Once before in the same year when the picture in the seashell frame had been taken and another drought plagued Burham. There had been no resurrection of Lady Tanfield that time. My Aunt Edith – Eira's mother – made us do the ritual a month after the drought began. Early enough that all it had taken was the sacrifice of a young hind to stop Lady Tanfield's return.

We had only been sixteen. The whole thing had been exciting and more than a little scary, but overall just a silly superstition – or so we'd thought until she rose fifteen years later. Four months ago today.

In unison, as we had on the hind, we pulled the knives through his flesh – hers southward and mine northward, until they met in the middle – to just below the bottom of his ribcage. His blood gushed across our hands and over our thighs as we knelt by him. The air filled with the rich tang of copper. I was not afraid or repulsed.

We put the knives aside and grasped the edges of the wound, pulling the skin back and open, revealing the thrumming crimson machinery of Mr. Tannis's body. He groaned, blood bubbling up past his lips, but he did not wake. I was hypnotized by the constant motion of his intestines, his stomach, his ribs. Eira leaned forward, her lips parted slightly, her eyes half closed. She forced one of her small hands up and under his ribcage, reaching farther and farther inside.

Mr. Tannis choked, arching up against the intrusion. The flowers fell from his eyelids, then he collapsed back, and went still as Eira ripped his heart from its aortic anchors and out, into the air. I reached for the lavender blossoms which lay in the dirt and was surprised that my hand wasn't shaking. I picked up the flowers and placed them on his eyelids once more.

The moon reached its peak and hung directly above the

ring of stones, above us. The blood that pooled around Mr.
Tannis was no longer red – it was liquid silver. His heart,
held aloft by Eira, seemed to glow in the intense light. Somewhere, another eldritch scream echoed through the night. She
lowered Mr. Tannis's heart to face level above his opened
torso. Our eyes met and, serenely, she dug her teeth into the
still twitching heart. I wondered how a human heart would
compare to that of a deer.

Eira's teeth ground back and forth, loosening the tough
muscle, before finally pulling a chunk free. She chewed
it slowly, her eyes now closed, and swallowed. Then she
offered it to me.

I glanced down at Mr. Tannis. His skin was paler, his
lips slightly parted, but he looked peaceful. Out of respect, I
reached with both hands and cradled his heart with as much
care as I could. It was warmer than I had expected. Almost
hot. This was the heart with which he had loved his brother
so fiercely. Perhaps he had not intended for it to be used in
this way but it would not go to waste.

I closed my eyes and pressed my lips against it. The
unholy creature by the river howled but its cry was cut short
as I dug my teeth into the heart of Mr. Tannis.

It was tougher than the heart of the hind we'd eaten
when we were sixteen, but somehow it felt more intimate
to eat Mr. Tannis's. Maybe because I had known him, had
seen him shout and fight, apologize and cry. I swallowed
and passed it back to Eira. Together we continued this way,
taking turns with the heart until we ate it completely and
licked the tepid blood from our fingers. By that time, the
sky was lighter, dawn painted the eastern horizon with faint

golds, bronzes, and topazes. I stood on shaking legs and helped Eira up. We both swayed, exhausted from our ritual. But there was one more job to do.

As one, we reached down and each grabbed one of Mr. Tannis's arms.

The low, dark clouds rolled in around two in the afternoon. They wreathed Burham in a false twilight and sent everyone running indoors as a heavy rain came crashing down. I was caught in it as I was biking to the Buckhead. As I ran in, soaking wet, George put a hot toddy on the bar for me.

"Looks like a good storm, that one," he said with a nod, as I sipped the hot beverage.

I was too weary to say anything, mourning for a man now buried beneath a new section of Eira's garden, his body given yet another use.

"Our guest checked out early this morning," George said, polishing a glass. "Guess he went back to Birmingham. Should anyone come round, I know the Chief will say he saw him driving back in the wee hours."

I nodded and finished my drink. Without saying anything more, George put another in front of me.

"On the house," he said. "The town's treating you today."

The storm lasted until midnight that night and two days later came a smaller storm, though still drenching. The Windrash swelled and frothed, drowning its own banks for a few hours, making the farmers who had fields around it a little nervous for a bit until it went down.

Standing in the open door of the station, I watched the large raindrops shatter against the cobblestone and then feed into the miniature rivers that ran between them. I wasn't too surprised at the ferocity of these surprise storms. The rain that the gentle deer had brought fifteen years ago had been soft and warm. Mr. Tannis's rain fell as he had lived: powerful, passionate, and raging.

The day the storms finally subsided, a week or so after the ritual, I returned to Eira's farm. When I pulled up, she was in her garden again – the new section – planting roses. She stood when she heard me and ran lightly through the wet grass in bare, muddy feet, embracing me in a tight hug. I relaxed in her strong arms, feeling safe, feeling calm again. The drought was over and, when she pulled back, I gave her the seashell framed photo with its new glass front.

Buried Two Feet Above

It was definitely a bad habit to take afternoon naps in a coffin. In my defense, I built them custom myself for people with eccentric tastes and who wanted to be buried in style, which meant I knew each one would be comfy as hell. Plus, my workshop wasn't built for creature comforts. I had some wooden benches, tables, a two-foot-tall base upon which I built the coffins, tons of tools and machinery, wood, and material. Not much there to enable me to chill on my lunch break. So, I started taking a little nap here and there, then it became a regular thing. Hey, I was my own boss.

But I certainly regret doing it now.

I pushed against the satin lined lid. It gave just enough that a crack of afternoon light sliced through the darkness, but not enough to let me force my hand into the space or get enough of a view to see what was preventing me from getting out or what had slammed the lid shut on me to begin with. I did thank my luck that I hadn't propped my foot up on the edge like I sometimes do. The lid would have smashed right on my ankle, though – perhaps – it would have allowed me to get out.

I let the lid sink down again and was swallowed by the dark. I cast my mind back. I thought I could remember a great crash. No earthquakes around here, but something had to have happened. My mind jumped to the latest shipment of oak planks I had gotten for my next custom order. I'd had the delivery guys prop them up against my back wall. If they fell, they could have landed directly on the coffin in which I now was trapped.

I tried to pull my legs up, knowing full well there wasn't enough space to brace my feet against the lid. I pressed my hands against the satin and shoved it over and over again, hoping to shake the timber off. I kept at it until my shoulders burned, then I let my hands fall across my chest in some messed-up parody of a trapped Dracula.

My heart raced and I tried to control my breathing. I wasn't afraid of being in a coffin, not one above ground that I had built myself at least. I remembered a piece of trivia I'd learned when I first got into the industry: how, in Victorian times, people were buried with bells in case their quack of a doctor said they were dead when they were actually just in a coma. I laughed and was a little spooked at the high-pitched sound of my own fear.

I broke it down. I worked independently so there were no coworkers or bosses to notice this little OSHA violation.

My studio was also in the empty field behind my house so screaming was pointless. No girlfriend to check in on me either.

Doubt my friends would notice my absence for quite a while. I was quite the introvert after all. Final nail in this coffin was that my client wouldn't be coming by to see the finished product until next month.

I sucked in a deep breath and held it. Can't panic. Panicking would do nothing.

I pushed the lid up again and craned my neck, peeking through the crack. I don't know what I was expecting to see. The light streaming in the windows was that mellow, warm glow of late afternoon. More than anything, I did not want to be here all night.

Gritting my teeth, I tried to shove my fingers into the narrow space but gave up with a curse when I felt the nail of my left index finger catch on an uneven edge and get pushed back. I forced myself to relax. My finger throbbed like a son of a bitch now.

I flinched at a small tickle on my ankle and tried rub both ankles together to rid myself of the sensation. It stopped then resumed. I tried to reach down before remembering where I was and swore again. The tickle was back and moving up my calf.

I pressed the lid up again and tucked my chin to my chest, squirming to try and see down the length of my body.

There, clinging to my leg hairs and its black carapace catching the light like a spark, was a small scorpion. I froze. It paused, its stinger raised a bit above its body. I swear it was staring at me. My arms shook in their awkward raised position. It lowered its left pincer to my skin. I repressed a shudder. I didn't want to give the little bastard any reason to sting me.

I tried to pull up any knowledge I had about scorpions. The bigger ones were the most poisonous? Or maybe it was based on colour? I was shocked out of my own thoughts as the scorpion did something very…unnatural.

It stroked my skin.

I felt my eyes bug out of my skull.

Deliberately, the scorpion ran its black pincer back and forth over my skin. I was so distracted that I let the lid slam shut. I heard something shift above me.

josssseph

I shoved at the lid and looked down. The scorpion hadn't moved but I'd heard something.

I'd heard something that sounded very much like my name.

My arms were getting weak from the constant tension of bracing the lid. The scorpion and I held our stalemate until I had to relent, letting the lid down gently so as not to scare it.

jossseph

I tried not to laugh with relief. I was saved. Someone had come in the shop.

"Hello? Hey! I'm in here, can you give me a hand? Hey! Right in the coffin!"

ah, joseph. you smell ssso good

I felt the scorpion scuttle up my leg a bit and I pushed the lid up again, my heart thundering in my throat.

It paused just below my knee, underneath the hem of my shorts. It lowered a pincer again, running it over my skin. Was this some kind of scouting behaviour? Checking for danger or some shit? Or maybe this little guy had a parasite that was making it act against its normal habits? Like that parasite that turned ants into visual nightmares and forced them to climb to the top of flowers so birds would eat them?

I turned my head to peek out.

"Hey! Who's there? I'm in this coffin, can you get me out, please?"

I couldn't see anyone. The light had lost its afternoon gold and was now shifting into dimmer evening hues. I looked back at my unwanted guest. If it kept climbing, I could have a chance to smash it with a fist. It seemed to only move if it was dark so I would have to close the lid.

I lowered the lid. My shoulders and wrists were aching. It was a relief to let them rest. I tried to ignore the pain so I could concentrate on the faint sensation on my knee.

such sssweet flesh

The sensation on my leg, it felt more like the soft caress of fingers than the skitter of a bug. Moreso, I would swear I felt the soft heat of someone's breath breeze across my knee and up my thigh. And the weight on the lower half of my legs… like someone was laying across them.

jossseph

I pushed the lid up again. The light that trickled inside was significantly dimmer, but it was enough so I could see the scorpion hadn't moved and – of course – there was no one else in the coffin with me. How would there be? I'd only built it with room for one.

The scorpion waited so I closed the lid again. I needed to get this over with now before night fell.

i can hear your heart, dear one, i can feel the blood beneath your sssskin

"Is anyone out there?" I called out, resisting the urge to lift the lid.

The scorpion finally made its move. First its prickly legs were distinct, then the sensation changed again and once more felt like a coquettish caress, sliding up my inner thigh so, so slowly.

ah, i am so glad i have you, i've been ssso lonely

A soft weight resting on my left hip, the whisper of an exhale not my own.

A shiver ran up my body from my toes to the top of my scalp and I shoved the lid up. A weak gray twilight seeped in. The scorpion waited on my hip, just where I thought I'd felt a hand. My skin erupted in goosebumps. I judged the distance. I could try. It would be hard to get a decent momentum considering the lack of space, if I didn't kill it then it might sting me. Holding the lid up solely with my right hand, I slid my left along the satin on the lid towards the scorpion. In response to my movement, the arachnid brought its wicked stinger high.

I waited, thinking it might relax after a few moments of stillness but it didn't back down. I could sense a terribly aware intelligence emitting from the scorpion. It stayed tense, stinger raised and ready. I pulled my hand back, dropping it to my chest in a tense fist. The scorpion waited then relaxed, its stinger sinking to a non-defensive pose.

I held the lid up still, clinging to the dimming twilight as desperately as I clung to my own hope that this nightmare would soon end. I tried to imagine possible positive outcomes. I would manage to crush it – maybe it would crawl into my armpit and then the danger would be gone.

Maybe Agatha would show up a month early to see her coffin and get me out of this mess, maybe I forgot to pay a bill and someone would come looking for cash, anything, anything better than imagining me starving to death in this fucking coffin or being stung and turning into a bloated corpse thanks to my little friend.

My arm was shaking so I let the lid close.

In the black void that was the inside of the coffin, I felt the scorpion make its way from my hip upwards to my waist. I should have been able to feel its tiny little horrible legs. I should have. Instead I felt a hand delicately slip up inside the bottom of my shirt.

oooohh, josssseph. yes. you're tender, aren't you. i feel your heart quickening…yesss

"Oh, God." I was shivering and couldn't stop it now.

It was a chain reaction. My body was now out of my control and I was terrified if I couldn't control it, the scorpion would get spooked and sting me. Why couldn't I remember what kind of scorpions were deadly? I pushed up the lid and barely noticed a difference between the darkness within the coffin and the light from outside. This was not good. Fuck.

i've watched you, oh yessss, i've been waiting

"Who's out there?"

My voice came out like a pathetic squeak. The phantom hand crept up, under my shirt, becoming uncomfortably intimate with my belly, then up towards my chest. I shoved the lid up, but it didn't matter anymore. It was night. Outside the coffin was just as dark as inside. There was nothing I could do at this point.

I felt a breath on my neck as the pressure slid across my chest, my collarbone, around my neck. A weight settled on my legs, my belly, like someone laying on top of me.

"Please. Please, whoever you are, don't do this." Who was I pleading with?

ah, yesss, right here. i feel it, oh, yesss

Something caressed my neck. My pulse pounded and this sensation was tracing it, too intimate, too vulnerable, I was about to lose it. It was the scorpion, climbing up my neck. What was that statistic? People ate eight spiders in their lifetime, in one night? I don't know. Was it going to end up in my mouth? Maybe that was for the best. I could crush it with my teeth, but what if it crawled over my eye, what if I didn't close it in time and its prickly little legs pierced my pupil? Oh fuck, oh fuck.

Chilled fingers closed around my throat. Weight shifted on my waist, grinding against me, hinting at something intimate yet carrying a more sinister meaning.

josssseph, oh yessss. The sssound of your pulsssse against me...you want me too, you were meant for me

The sensation gripped my neck tighter, not enough to cut off air, but enough to make my heart race. It took everything not to start thrashing. Any move could set the scorpion off. I felt a warm breath against my neck, the tickle of lips on my right ear. I was losing it. This had to be insanity.

"Is anyone out there?" I croaked.

In response, I heard a breathy giggle in my ear.

i am here for you, josssseph. yes. right here. tell me, sssay you want thisss

I couldn't even make a sound. My throat felt swollen

with a captured scream. There was someone else. Someone laying across the length of my body. No, no, no. I was alone. I was in a coffin. There was only room for one.

I only built it with room for one.

i want to kissss you, jossseph. yesss, that's allowed, issn't it?

I felt the weight shift on my body and a short breath exhaled over my face that smelled dry, like the desert. I parted my lips, this was my moment to scream, my last moment. Lips as smooth and dry as parchment pressed against mine, something slipped between my lips and into my mouth like a desert snake. I felt a slight sting. A momentary blink of pain.

I was clutching at the air above my body – there was no one there, no one there.

My body began to numb, my neck was throbbing, where were my legs? I couldn't feel them. The void crept through my veins, my fingers were gone, my arms and chest went next. Was this it? Was this it?

clossse your eyesss. breath me in. oh, josssseph

Why not? I closed my eyes. It was darkness either way. I closed them and felt adrift in a numbing nothingness. I felt my heart-rate slow when it should have been racing. My breaths dragged in and out…in…and out….in…and…out…

I was breathing through my mouth. I could taste sand. I could taste dry air. I could taste sunshine.

give yoursssself to me, i want you sssso bad, joseph

yes. i will give myself to her
it
her
i'll do it
it's dark and I feel
weak
my arms
my
legs
i'm floating
and so i gave myself to her
it
and just
let go

GODMOUTH

The first time I heard it was from a dying woman's lips. She'd been hit by a car that had been going at least double the speed limit. The driver hadn't stopped. Instead, the car squealed around a corner and disappeared as the woman slammed into the ground with a sickening crunch. I saw it happen, as did four other strangers.

I ran to the woman's side as she lay dying. I knew she had to be. I was a nurse and the amount of blood surrounding the woman on the pavement was gruesome. I heard a man on his cellphone, talking to the 911 dispatch.

The other strangers stood a little ways away, watching as I checked her vitals and tried to make her comfortable. Her eyes were a beautiful shade of the palest green, reflecting the stormy sky above. She wasn't upset or crying. I thought that she must be in shock.

"Miss, an ambulance is coming," the man on the cell-phone said, raising his voice to avoid coming closer.

I nodded.

"Did you hear that? Just hold on, you'll be okay," I lied, pressing my scarf against the deep gash on her scalp.

Half of her forehead had been scraped up and into her hairline from her collision with the pavement. Her skull glistened. Her lips moved but I couldn't hear any sound coming from them. Her eyes never left the sky. In the distance, I heard the insistent wail of an ambulance. I leaned in, turning my head so my ear was closest to her mouth. I heard the faint whisper of the breath, she was trying to say something. The ambulance screamed through the streets.

"Is there anything I can do? Is she going to be alright?" a woman asked, clutching her coat around her and staring at me with wide, frightened eyes.

I shook my head and turned back to the dying woman. I started. She was staring right at me. Her manicured hand clutched at my sleeve and she smiled. I leaned in, meaning to comfort her.

"Godmouth," she said.

She died then. Her fingers slipped from my sleeve to land in her blood, which was reflecting the sky as her eyes did once more. There was a content smile on her lips.

"May she rest in peace," said another woman, shaking her head.

"Such a shame," said the woman clutching her coat.

"Did anyone get that asshole's license plate?" said the man.

The ambulance roared around the corner and rolled to a

stop nearby. I stood and stepped away from the dead woman as the EMTs jumped out of the back. The others and I stood and watched them try to resuscitate her. It wasn't long before they gave up and put the body on a stretcher and covered those blank eyes with a blanket.

The women crept close, their eyes latched onto the still figure underneath the cover. The EMTs called in the death. A police car finally rolled up.

"What did she say to you?" asked one of the women.

"Did she know that asshole in the car?" asked the other.

I shook my head.

"Godmouth," I said.

"God?" repeated the first woman.

"She was praying," said the other.

Satisfied, the women drifted off together to talk to the police. I thought about what they had said. It hadn't sounded like a prayer.

By the time I finished giving my statement and information to the police, it was growing late. I watched the police car and ambulance slowly pull away, all the strangers and watchers turned and wandered away as well.

Only the blood pool on the pavement remained. I stared at the reflection of the clouds on the blood, at my stained scarf lying next to it, before turning my back against it all and walking home.

The next time, I didn't hear it. Rather I saw it written on the side of a building in egg yellow spray paint next to a crude representation of a wide open mouth with square teeth hanging out. It was written all as one word:

GODMOUTH

I caught sight of it as I was walking to the hospital. I stopped at the mouth of the alley and stared into the shadows. It'd been written at chest height, above some dented trashcans. It was the first time I thought about that woman in two days.

I took out my phone and stepped into the alley, trying to avoid the puddles of vomit and piss, garbage and what looked suspiciously like human shit. I didn't know why but I wanted a picture of the graffiti. After I snapped two pictures of it, I stood and stared at it. I felt a chill come over me as I remember the dead woman's smile and the way her beautiful green eyes had reflected the clouds, how she had whispered that final word in such a calm and loving way.

I was brought back to the present by the stench of a homeless man who had come up behind me.

"Spare a dollar for a homeless vet?" He coughed into his dirty hands before holding one out to me.

I dug a couple dollars out of my coat pocket and handed them to him, escaping as his attention was turned to counting them out. I drew my new scarf tighter around my neck and hurried down the sidewalk, dodging the business men and women in fashionable clothes as they left work.

I reached the hospital a few minutes late and my supervisor chewed me out as I got into my scrubs. I followed my boss out as she continued her rant.

"I can't have my nurses coming in late," Ellen said as she charged down the crowded hallway. "You know how hectic and swamped we can be. I expect more from you, you're one of the best nurses I have. Things have been crazy these last few weeks, you should know better."

"I'm sorry, Ellen. I won't let it happen again."

"No, you won't," she replied, shoving a clipboard at me.

I looked over the counter of the nurse's station at the crowded waiting room. All the seats were taken and even more people leaned against the walls or slouched in groups near the entrance.

"No time to just stand around," Ellen said as she sat down in the chair behind the counter and began to sort through the forms there.

I turned and went back down the hall to where the elevators were. The elevator dinged just as I pressed the 'up' button. I stood aside as Jimmy, a night orderly, wheeled out an old man. The gentleman was withered, slouched over his lap with thick ropes of drool dangling from his mouth. He smelled distinctly of urine and, from the dark patch on his crotch, it was obvious where the smell was coming from. Jimmy saw my expression and nodded.

"Yeah, I'll clean him up. It happened on the way down and I need to get him to the MRI. He was fine an hour ago, talking about politics. So bizarre."

The old man began to rock back and forth. I saw a smile on his face and then he said it:

GODMOUTH

I flinched and stared. "What did he say?"

Jimmy looked down at the smiling, drooling old man and shrugged.

"I don't know what it means, he just keeps saying it. Probably a side effect of the stroke he had or whatever it is that caused this." Jimmy lifted a hand in a wave as he pushed the wheelchair down the hall and away from me.

Staring after them, I stepped onto the elevator and pressed the button for the fifth floor. Ellen was obviously pissed at me since she had given me the worst night duty to cover: the psych ward. Normally this was covered by the resident psych doctors but, with budgets cuts, it had been relegated to the nurses. On the bright side, they usually always assigned two nurses to take care of the patients since some of them could be violent.

Alison was already behind the counter on the fifth floor, waiting for me to arrive so we could start the rounds. Alison was my favourite person to be teamed up with. She was forty but acted like she was still in college, cracking dirty jokes and partying on her days off. Ellen hated her, which is why Alison often worked the night shift on the fifth floor. She smirked at me when she caught sight of me.

"Guess who got lucky last night?" she asked by way of a hello.

I rolled my eyes but couldn't help smiling.

"Let's see to our guests and you can tell me all about it," I replied.

She filled me in on all the sticky details as we walked the bright halls to the backdrop of whimpering, screaming, and hissed one-sided conversations. I hated this floor so much.

We rounded the final corner and she took the left side, I took the right. We peeked in the windows, checking to make sure everyone was in bed, or at least, accounted for. Most of these people weren't too unstable, just some mild schizophrenia and paranoia.

Occasionally, they could get violent but neither of us would be actually going in the rooms. I was checking the third room when I froze. The patient, Walter Carson, was asleep with his back to me. Above his bed, scrawled in big, blocky letters was the word that had been haunting me.

GODMOUTH

Worse, the words were wet looking and red. I must have gasped because Alison was immediately at my side.

"Oh Jesus, Mary, and Joseph. Is that blood?"

"I think so," I said.

"Fuck me, is he dead? That's a lot of blood. Is he breathing? Can you tell if he is breathing?"

I squinted through the window but shook my head.

"We have to go in there," I said.

"I'm calling security."

Alison darted down the hall to the nurse's station.

I found my hand on the doorknob before I realized what I was doing. Alison argued with someone on the phone as I stepped inside the room, leaving the door open behind me so the hall light could shine further into the room. The words glared out through the shadows, gleaming in the faint light. Inside the room, I saw that the opposite wall had been marked as well.

The crude mouth drawing, exactly the same as the one in the alley, had been dabbed onto the wall with more blood. This drawing was larger though and I could make out that the teeth were long and stretched down past the lower lip. They ended in a blunt line, not in points like I would have assumed.

I'd completely forgotten the patient until I found a roughly made shiv at my throat. I froze.

"You see? You see?" the patient muttered, his other hand

rising to point at the painting.

I could see his hand was coated with tacky blood. His wrist had been gashed open. He pulled me to the open door.

"I need to leave. I am needed. I must spread the word."

We stepped into the light and I saw Alison standing next to a security guard.

Her mouth was agape as she stared at us. I wanted to say something, scream even, but I was frozen, my lips felt numb. I felt my knees shook and suddenly I knew I was going to faint and that, when I did, the knife would slice my throat as I fell against it.

My chest seized up, caught in the tight bands of panic that threatened to take control. I clenched my fists and allowed my nails to bite into the skin, hoping the pain would clear my head. Alison was speaking, trying to calm the patient. I felt him shake his head behind me.

"I must leave. I must. Open the doors. Open them. I need to leave. I am needed. Look and see!" He pointed into his room.

The security guard took a step forward. The patient growled, grabbing my hair and pulling my head back and exposing my throat.

"No, no, no, no, no!" he screamed.

I saw the hand with the blade rise and I tried to bring my hands up to stop him but they moved so slow, as though in a dream. The patient jerked against me and his hand fell away from my hair as he slumped to the ground. I looked over my shoulder and saw another security guard with a gun raised. I hadn't even heard the shot.

I stumbled away from the patient and leaned against the wall, trying to catch my breath. My ears rang. I watched

Alison kneel next to the man and check for a pulse. She shook her head and a security guard radioed the information back downstairs.

Soon, I was heading down myself. Ellen waited for me in her office. I sat down before her and took the tea she offered. It was Ellen's method. She wanted to be liked by everyone on the staff but she couldn't help being the controlling bitch that she was. So she made me this tea to seem like she cared that I had almost had my throat cut by some psycho, but I could tell by the deep lines around her eyes that she was more angry than concerned.

"I'm glad you're alright," she lied.

I nodded and waited for the axe to drop.

"I can understand that you were concerned for the patient, which made you enter that room without waiting for security. However, now a patient is dead. We have rules for a reason."

I nodded again, staring into the steaming mug.

"Normally, I would put you on an unpaid suspension but we're short-staffed as is. I'll just have you give you a written warning and put this incident in your file. I hope you will learn from this. You've gotten sloppy and I can't have patients dying because of your lack of due diligence," Ellen cleared her throat and stood. "Of course, I am glad you are okay. You may go."

By the time I'd returned to the fifth floor, a janitor had cleaned the blood off the walls and floor. Alison was waiting in tense silence at the nurse's station. I was glad when day broke and the shift ended. Listening to those people scream and cry and whisper all night made me feel like I'd be locked up next.

Walking home, I saw more graffiti. It was everywhere, as if an army of madmen had swamped the city armed with spray paint. I saw shop owners scraping the words off their windows with fast, angry movements, a businessman throwing a fit over his vandalized Mercedes that now had a new mouth painted on the hood. I saw the words in chalk on the sidewalk, in paint on walls, and written with marker on the sides of buses. I was glad to finally get home.

My fiancé, Rob, had already left for work. I checked the fridge to see if he'd left me any notes but found none. I showered. Even after scrubbing and scrubbing, I could still feel the patient's hand in my hair and his homemade knife at my throat but I couldn't remember his name. I was too awake to even try falling asleep so I turned on the TV, hoping the sound would make me feel safe again.

I was in an endless black field. Or, maybe it was an ocean. It churned and rose and fell. But it wasn't an ocean and it wasn't a field. It was something awful and I didn't want to see what it was. It was massive, it went on forever, it was all around me. I didn't want to see, I didn't want to but I couldn't close my eyes to it. I felt it closing in all around me and I opened my mouth to scream.

I woke with a violent start and found the TV blaring fake applause as a contestant correctly guessed an answer. I pulled myself up into a sitting position and checked the time.

It was just past six. A voicemail waited for me on my cell. It was Rob, telling me he was going to be late.

I shivered and looked out over the back of the couch. The apartment was dark and empty. I went to the kitchen, turning on all the lights as I went. I doubled checked my work schedule on the fridge and was relieved to see that I was off for the next two days.

A heavy feeling of sadness hung over me, whether from the incident with the patient or from that fast fading dream I'd had, I couldn't tell. I didn't want to be alone. I tried calling Rob to see when he would be home but only got his voicemail. I tried calling a few friends and when none picked up, I felt this certain knowledge that everyone in the world must have disappeared while I slept. Disappeared into that vast darkness. I clutched at the counter, overwhelmed with that sudden wave of irrational panic.

The sharp, shrill jangle of my phone caused me to scream with fright even as I grabbed it in relief. It was Rob calling me back.

"Sorry babe, I know I'm running late. The CIO, CEO, and a bunch of managers didn't come into work today and no one can seem to get a hold of them. It's been chaos here. I'm just leaving now, let's meet at The Cookery tonight, my treat, huh?"

I wanted to ask him to come get me. That I was too shaken to walk to the restaurant three blocks away but I held it in and just said yes. I got dressed and pulled on my jacket. Through the apartment walls, I could hear the TV of my neighbours. It felt like, with Rob's call, the world and all its cacophony had come back again.

Wrapping my scarf around my neck, I left my apartment building and turned down the dim street. All around me, the words stood out in sickly yellow paint.

Despite being a Friday night, the sidewalks weren't filled with people going to bars or restaurants or clubs as they usually were. The men and women I did see walked at a quick pace – almost a jog – clutching their purses or scarves tight as they rushed to get wherever they were going. Most kept their faces turned down to the ground beneath their feet but others were like me and stared at the word that marked almost every surface.

I heard the crisp crinkle of paper under my feet and looked down. I'd trampled a pamphlet. As I stepped off it, I stopped. Looking up at me in neat black ink was the mouth. Numb, I reached down and picked it up. In a simple font, GODMOUTH was printed across the top in capital letters. Then, underneath, was a detailed drawing of the mouth. Now I could see that what I had thought were teeth were really thick segmented tentacles that draped down from the spherical mouth.

I opened the pamphlet, hoping for an explanation but found only nonsensical gibberish. Over and over the words were printed, sometimes in capitals, sometimes in lower case. Spread throughout were sentences like GRANT US PEACE, RELEASE US, CLEANSE, PURIFY, ERASE, and WE ARE ALL EQUAL INSIDE.

I looked on the back for a printer's logo and found only blank paper. I let the pamphlet drop and wiped my hand on my pants. Continuing on my way, I saw that the sidewalk was littered with those pamphlets for blocks.

I walked by an open alleyway and heard wailing laughter. I paused and looked in. Five young men and a woman stood in a circle around another woman who was kneeling in the refuse before them. It looked like they were carving something into her forehead with a small pocket knife. The woman looked over at me, said something to the others, and they all turned.

I could see what they had carved into the woman's forehead clearly now because they had already done it to themselves. It was a rough copy of the mouth, standing out crimson with their blood. The woman with the freshly gashed brand smiled as the blood ran down her face. The men leered and began to walk toward me. I turned and ran. Their laughter chased me.

I didn't stop until I was inside The Cookery. Rob waited at a table next to one of the front windows. I sat in one of the wicker chairs, the pristine tablecloth rustling against my legs. A tea candle in a pink glass holder flickered between us.

"Hey, sweetie." He reached over and clasped my hand in his. I looked down at my hand in his as I tried to catch my breath.

"Hey, are you alright?" He made as though to stand but I waved him down again.

In short, choppy sentences, I told him what had happened in the alley on the way here. His face went ashen.

"Jesus, I'm so sorry. I should have picked you up, especially with what has been going on lately."

I looked at him and he must have seen the confusion in my face.

"It's been all over the news. They think there's some

new gang or something. It's so strange though. I mean, normally gangs tend to stick to an age range or nationality but the members of this gang range from all over."

The waiter walked over and Rob ordered for the both of us. We only ever got the same thing each time we came here: the Konnichiwa Hotdog with wasabi mayo, all beef sausage, bacon, tempura bits, and mayo for Rob and the Bishop Burger with bacon, cheese, panko crusted fried shrimp, the secret sauce, lettuce, and extra pickles for me. Both came with the house special sweet potato fries fried in duck fat. It was all sinfully delicious.

"I haven't heard anything about that," I said, picking at my napkin and tearing bits and pieces off of it.

"I'm not surprised, you never pick up a newspaper and you sleep through the news." Rob laughed.

"Tell me about it then." I wanted to hear him say the word. I wanted to see if it was haunting him like it was me.

"I don't know. They just suddenly appeared, I guess. They don't seem to be involved in drugs or any illegal activity really, besides the fact that they are vandalizing everything they can. One of them got my boss's car two days ago, he was pissed." Rob laughed again.

"What – what are they writing?"

Rob shrugged and leaned back as the server brought over our beers, placing them on the table with two solid thunks.

"I don't know, the name of their gang or something. Me and the guys think they're some sort of cult like Marilyn Manson's group or whatever."

"Charles Manson," I muttered.

"What?"

I shrugged. I was disappointed. How could he forget that word? Didn't it haunt him too?

GODMOUTH

"A cult makes more sense really. Especially what you said about those fucking kids cutting into their foreheads."

I nodded and looked out onto the street. It was empty now. The twilight grew thicker, darker. One by one, streetlights flashed on, flooding the street with weak yellow light. One illuminated a mouth drawn on the shop window of a boutique across the street.

"There's no one out tonight," I said.

"What?" Rob looked out, absently, his eyes glazed over in thought. "Oh, they're probably out on Deusore Street or something."

"I doubt it. I think all the sane ones are locked up safely in their homes, hoping to wait out whatever is on its way."

We were both surprised at what I'd said. Rob looked at me long and hard with a worried glint in his eyes. I tried to smile, try to make it seem all like a little joke. Then the server brought us our food, steaming on white porcelain plates and looking like heaven. It gave us an excuse not to talk.

Sunday was bright and beautiful. It was usually the only day we both had off since I normally worked Saturdays. As a treat, Rob had ordered a gourmet picnic from some little shop on Deusore Street and we went to Warden Row Park for lunch. Even though the day was unseasonably warm and the birds sang in the branches above our heads, I felt ill-at-ease.

Rob was as oblivious as ever, in fact, he was even happy. He was convinced that the missing managers meant he'd be getting a promotion soon. He'd hated the missing CIO most of all since he worked directly underneath him. For Rob, everything was looking up.

But I'd seen the people hidden in the alleys, hunched over distinct pamphlets. I'd seen that word everywhere. It crowded out shop windows and blanketed walls, sidewalks, cars. The mouth gaped on stop signs and benches. The city was being swamped. Even the park was not untouched. I'd seen it on the beautiful fountain, the ugly word smeared on it like yellowed feces. Looking at it made me feel dizzy.

"I think I have a good chance at it," Rob was saying, smiling.

"Hey, look at the fountain. Do you see that?" I pointed.

His brow furrowed. He turned and I watched the back of his head. I watched the wind caress his curls.

"I don't know, it's some graffiti." He turned back, shrugging.

"Yeah, but what does it say? I'm curious," I lied.

He glanced over his shoulder for a moment and then picked through the basket to grab another croissant.

"Who cares? Some shithead wrote something dumb."

I stared past him. I could clearly read it.

GODMOUTH

It screamed at me from across the grass.

"Don't you think, honey?" Rob asked and I nodded with a smile.

The day seemed to darken. I looked up into the sky, squinting against the stark daylight. There were no clouds but still there seemed to be a looming darkness that hovered over the city. And yet the sun still shone as if it wasn't there.

"More cheese?"

I shook my head.

Suddenly, I knew we were being watched. I jerked my head and stared back over my shoulder. A woman turned away and bent down to pick up her dog's crap. Beyond her, a man sat on a bench reading the newspaper. I turned my head back and looked beyond Rob. A couple walked by, holding hands. A mother pushed a stroller.

"Hey! Hey!" Rob snapped his fingers in front of my eyes.

I looked at him.

"Jesus, where are you today?"

"Sorry, I guess I thought I heard something."

He studied me. I was relieved when his phone rang. I knew I would have to tell him about the word, about my experience with the dead woman, and the crazed patient. I'd point out the graffiti, the gaping mouth, the pamphlets that littered the streets. But would he think I was crazy?

Rob hung up and grinned. "They want me in on Monday to talk about the position. I told you, I told you I was next up!"

I smiled along with him. We walked home together holding hands and I watched as he carefully stepped over the pamphlets without really realizing he was doing it. We walked past a dozen or so fresh graffiti marks. I didn't point them out.

After we made love, I dreamed of that dark expanse that wanted to devour me.

I looked all around me and heard others but could not see them. I called out Rob's name but did not hear him. It was closing in. Those dark, moist folds of darkness would wrap around me, and then what?

I woke as Rob pushed himself out of bed, turning off his obnoxious alarm. I felt fuzzy, things seemed out of focus. I tried to go back to sleep as he showered but couldn't.

"Wish me luck, babe." Rob tightened his tie and grinned.

I did so and watched him leave. I spent the day on the couch, watching TV. Normally, I used my days to visit shops, cafes, wherever I wanted but I saw that the streets were still empty this morning as they had been over the weekend. I didn't want to go out there into the silence. I imagined how oppressing the quiet would be, how unnerving the emptiness. I thought of the group of kids in the alley, carving simplistic gaping mouths into their foreheads and shuddered.

So I watched the news instead.

"Police sergeant Roger Morris finally gave a statement regarding this new gang that some citizens have dubbed 'The Mouthers'," the pretty petite newscaster chirped.

The camera cut to an overweight, graying man in uniform leaning with a weary heaviness against a desk littered with crushed Styrofoam cups, coffee rings, and scattered papers. A crowd of reporters crowded him, microphones jabbing at his face.

"All I have to say is that the situation is being handled. This is not a serious issue."

"What about the recent triple homicide? Weren't the victims brutalized with the image of the mouth carved into their chests?" a reporter shouted over the others.

"Can you comment on the recent massive amount of disappearances in the city?" Another reporter pushed forward.

The sergeant wiped his face and slumped further down against the desk.

"All I can say at this time is that the disappearances have not been exclusively linked to any one event or group."

"What about the murders? Isn't it true the homicide rate is on the rise?"

"I have no other comment at this time except to advise the citizens of this city to stay indoors after dark, keep their windows and doors locked, and to avoid any situation that might place them in danger."

The sergeant turned and waved away the bustling reporters that tried to surge after him. The camera cut back to the perky blonde.

"While the authorities won't confirm that the disappearances that have been on the rise are related to the recent cultish gang activity, I think it's safe to say that there must be some connection. Now, on to Myles with the weather."

I switched it then and let a talk show host scream about the wonders of the new diet pill she had discovered while I waited to go to work. Rob messaged me once, confirming that he'd gotten the promotion. I had to wonder if it was any sort of an accomplishment to get promoted just because your boss had disappeared. Probably running around naked with a mouth cut into his forehead, I thought to myself and shuddered.

I didn't relish the idea of walking to work in the empty streets as the sky dimmed but there were also no taxis in sight. I clutched my pepper spray in one hand and avoided all alley entrances, refusing to even look at them.

I arrived twenty minutes early, having practically run the last block after someone, somewhere, started shrieking. Ellen sat behind desk, her face buried in her hands. The waiting room was as empty and as quiet as the streets.

"Ellen?"

The older woman jumped and looked up with eyes surrounded by the smear of old mascara.

"Oh, it's you. Why did you bother coming in? There's no one here." Her lip trembled and I was shocked to see the glisten of fresh tears in her eyes.

Ellen was like iron, I'd never seen her scream or yell or cry. "Ellen?"

I reached out and touched her hand. Maybe she saw this as permission to be weak because she grabbed my hand and pressed her damp face against it, crying. I let her go on for a bit before pulling away. I circled around the desk and put my arm around her.

"What happened, Ellen? Where is everyone?"

She hiccupped and rallied, trying to put on the same mask she wore every day for her staff.

"Dead," she said and shrugged. "Or insane. This whole city seems to be going to shit."

Her lip trembled again and she bit it, drawing blood, "My – my Kevin. He went over, he lost it."

Her whole body began to shake and I pressed her tightly against me, trying to quell it.

"He brought home one of those ugly pamphlets." She stuck out a hand and opened it."He kept saying how this was the solution everyone needed but didn't know they needed it. Then he just left. He didn't even pack his bags. He was just gone. He left his cell phone, his wallet, all his money, and – and –"

A man's wedding ring glinted in the overhead fluorescent light. We both looked at it. The silence was heavy.

"Where are the other nurses, Ellen? Where are the patients?"

"Gone, I told you. Dead or …worse. Yesterday, when the sky went dark in the afternoon, everything went crazy."

I thought about my picnic and the sun that struggled to shine through a dark mass that wasn't there and yet, all the same, hovered over the entire city like a brief storm.

"Joe was killed," Ellen mumbled. "He tried to stop all the psych patients from leaving. You know how he is, always sticking he nose in and meddling. The patient from room 204, Sandy Mitchell, she stabbed Joe in the eye with a pen. I don't even know where she got it from."

I was afraid to ask.

"And Alison?"

Ellen shook her head.

"Alison never showed. She didn't answer her phone either. She's missed two shifts."

"Let's go, Ellen. You should go home."

"I can't." The woman broke down again. "It's so empty there and I keep thinking he's going to come back, but he doesn't and I'm so afraid."

So, I left her there in the empty hospital. The sun had fully set by then and some people were out. It was still so quiet. I pulled my pepper spray out of my purse again and made my way down the sidewalk. Several people had dried blood on their faces and clotted messes on their foreheads, where I assumed they'd carved mouths. Their eyes were raised to the sky, they smiled as if waiting for a great surprise. Others were like me, scared and twitchy.

Rob was on the couch, beer in hand, and watching TV when I stepped in.

"I thought you were at work," he said by way of a greeting.

"No one was there except Ellen. All the patients and staff were gone."

I felt numb, like I was walking through a dream and trying to figure out how to wake up.

"Yeah, we had a skeleton crew going on today too. It was exhausting having to deal with everything."

"The city is going insane."

He looked over at me, his eyes lit up by the light of the TV screen. "Why do you say that?"

"Are you blind? Don't you see the people walking around with mouths carved into their foreheads? Haven't you seen the pamphlets? The graffiti? It's – it's –" I struggled to say it but couldn't.

I tumbled helplessly to the couch beside him.

"Jesus, hun. You're starting to sound a little crazy yourself."

"You can't not see it! It's everywhere!"

He just looked at me, concern and even a little fear on his face. We sat side by side on the couch, an old Western playing while he nursed a beer and I tried to figure out if I was, in fact, going a little crazy. Beyond the tinny sounds of the movie, I felt the overwhelming and horrible silence of the city. It lay in wait for the pauses between words to creep forward like a living thing.

Later, after we'd brushed our teeth and Rob lay beside me, snoring, I listened for the silence between his breaths. I forced my clenched jaw to relax for the fifth time and forced my fists to open. I looked over and gazed out through the window. All the windows of the neighbouring building were dark. The air felt heavy, pressing down on me.

I thought of the dead woman who spoke the word into my life the very first time. She stared up into the sky with a smile on her face. I passed the time until I fell asleep in my memories. It felt safest there. Then I dreamed of nothing but darkness.

In the morning, I felt calm. I stood on our apartment balcony and leaned over the railing. Below I saw that the streets were full with people, it almost looked like a regular workday. Except that most of the people weren't rushing to get somewhere. Most of the people stood on the sidewalk or in the street, looking up to the cloudless sky. Most people waited.

Rob came up behind me, frowning as he stared down at his phone. I noticed a glaring yellow mouth painted across the side of the apartment building across the street. I wondered if I just hadn't noticed it yesterday or if someone had managed to do it just last night in the darkness.

"I got an email from work, they sent out a company-wide mass email. They told us not to bother coming in today."

"Makes sense."

He looked at me. I saw the fear in his eyes. He thought I was losing it but I wasn't. I shrugged and took his hand. I pulled him close against me and looked up. He looked up.

It began.

It started slow. The sky darkened for no reason. If you weren't expecting, you never would have noticed – not at first anyway. Then a great void yawned open, made up of coils of inky darkness, much like smoke. It stretched and stretched until it hung over the whole city. I heard the people on the street below gasp. The darkness solidified, became more real. In the void, I saw the great, convulsing folds take form. The darkness roiled with fearsome life.

Then four massive, thick tentacles emerged. They were segmented like that of a worm and were of a dusky, dark purplish colour that reminded me of a deep and old bruise. At the tips, the tentacles ended in a multitude of smaller, more flexible appendages that reached and twisted. The massive tentacles moved with a delicate and slow determination. I watched them stretch past buildings until I lost sight of the tips. I felt the impact though. Everyone did. Rob screamed and clutched at me, gripping the balcony railing with his other hand.

"It's an earthquake!" he cried.

He tried to pull me into the apartment but I shrugged him off. I finally realized. Rob couldn't see it. He thought it was an earthquake because he couldn't see the GODMOUTH. He was blind.

He pulled at my arm once before I jerked it away from him. I turned my back on him and stared up at the darkness. Car alarms blared, people screamed in the streets. I heard the apartment's front door slam shut.

I looked down and watched as Rob ran into the street, pushing those who stood still and calm, staring up. The tentacles strained. Their thick flesh bulged with the effort. Then GODMOUTH moved.

It pulled itself down. The sun was gone, a false twilight fell upon the city. I felt that I should be afraid but was not. Below, the streets surged with those who were blind to the vast entity that bore down on our city. The drivers drove with desperate frenzy, crashing into those who stood waiting and those others who also tried in vain to escape. The great lips widened, stretched around to encompass the entire city.

There was no escape. I turned and walked out of my apartment, but I did not descend the stairs as Rob had. Instead, I went to the roof. The roof door was unlocked, as always. I saw a few others from the building leaning against the railing, not talking or crying, just watching. I joined them. It was nice to be with people who understood.

Together, we watched GODMOUTH draw itself ever nearer. I felt the draw of the terrible emptiness between the black folds in the mouth. There was a place for me there. There was a place for all of us there and we would all be made equal. The man standing next to me took my hand. I did not look at him but I was grateful. My hand was cold, his was cold.

The great lips connected with the earth. The city was

now trapped beneath the dome that was GODMOUTH. No escape. All one could do now was wait. But that was alright. I was alright. In the end, it came quickly. A horrible heaviness came first, a crushing weight, pressing down with intent. Then the unnatural silence of a whole city frozen in anticipation. Those massive creeping, undulating folds came down upon us.

They opened up and at that moment, looking up at what awaited me, my numbness finally broke and I screamed.

CRIMSON SPLASHED SKIN

"Can you get me close?" I asked.

Kyle nodded, looking out over the rippling waves. The ocean was quiet, dark under a clouded sky.

"I think so. They sweep the water with spotlights every hour at random intervals, but they'll be looking for ships," he said.

He turned away from the view of the half dozen Navy vessels bobbing on the water, but I continued to stare at the black behemoths, wishing I'd brushed up on the different types of ships so I could identify what was out there. When I looked back at Kyle, he was pulling off his powder-blue polo, revealing an evenly tanned chest. He'd gained weight since I'd last seen him. Despite this, I still felt that familiar flutter in the bottom of my belly. I pulled off my t-shirt and kicked off my shorts, confident in my consistent dieting and gym routine. I relished his lustful stare as we stood on the sand.

"So, how do you plan on getting us past the U.S. Navy?"

"Surfboards."

My mouth gaped and Kyle smirked, pleased at having shocked me.

"It's overcast tonight," he said. "I've also covered the surfboards in black duct tape and we have black wetsuits. All of that should make it near impossible for them to spot us. We'll paddle out nice and quiet to the impact site, right under their noses,"

"Simple enough," I said. "I like it."

"Got your camera, Ms. Intrepid Reporter?"

"Waterproof and full batteries." I pulled it from the bag at my feet, putting the strap over my neck.

"Then let's go."

"Won't your wife wonder where you are?" I walked with him to the water's edge, where two surfboards were laid out.

"She's at home with the kids, probably binge-watching something, I'm not worried about it."

The water was painfully cold, lapping at my toes in hungry slurps. I pulled on the wetsuit, hoping for some warmth. The suit was too big for me, stretched out from years of use, but it would have to do. We picked up the surfboards and paddles, then waded in. The chill of the ocean caused me to shiver, but I relished it. It took my mind off the agony that was dinner earlier.

Despite how much Kyle had aged, how many pounds he'd put on, I still felt the powerful chemistry. The tension had been palpable. I hated the idea of how easily I would give myself to him, the one who got away, even when I had Carmen waiting for me at home.

I watched as he straddled his board in the water. He looked back at me once with a wry grin before dipping his paddle into the waves and began to cut towards the ships.

What I'd had with Kyle had been wild, violent even. Our sex had been a whirlwind of biting, hair-pulling, and scratching – a maelstrom of unfettered passion. I shook my head to clear it. I had Carmen waiting for me. Steady and safe Carmen. She was someone I could spend the rest of my life with.

I straddled my own board and paddled after Kyle. The ocean rolled beneath me in soft, easy hills. I was careful to dip my paddle quietly, avoiding any splashes. Sliding over the nighttime waters, time seemed to disappear. I counted three spotlight patrols in the time it took Kyle and me to creep up to the first ship. There was a heart-stopping moment when, during the third sweep, a spotlight had flashed over me. The brilliant beam blinded me and all the hair on my body had shocked straight up as I waited for the alarm.

When my vision came back, several agonizing minutes later, the night was quiet. I allowed my heart to slow before resuming my journey. Soon, we began to pass the ships. Overhead, I could hear the faint conversations of the officers on deck and the constant humming of the machinery within the hulls. When another sweep began, we were safe, being so close to the vessels themselves. The spotlights roamed across the waves looking for other boats, not tiny surfboards. It was almost too easy getting past their watch.

Out on the endless ocean, with the beach a thin strip

behind me, I felt my heart pounding in my chest. I was excited beyond words. Overhead, the thick cloud cover hung heavy over my head like a funerary shroud. Kyle had stopped and I slid up beside him. Even just the brush of his knee against mine gave me a thrill.

"Shit, I can't feel my legs!" I whispered, trying to distract myself.

"There it is," he said, looking ahead.

I followed his gaze. Almost invisible in the dense darkness was a great, winding pillar, twisting up out of the water and into the heavens. It rose at least forty feet above the waterline. From this distance, it looked black without texture or any defining features. I knew I would have to get closer. Without saying anything to Kyle, I paddled onwards.

As time passed, out on those gentle waves, the clouds began to thin. A watery light poured down from the bloated moon and illuminated the aberration in front of me. Even with the light as weak as it was, I started to discern the details of the pillar. I wanted to get clear photos, so I got closer and closer, until I was just a few feet away. Kyle pulled out a tiny penlight, shining its thin beam onto the surface of the obelisk.

I grabbed my camera in both hands, tightening my thighs around the edges of the surfboard to steady my shots. I used the flash, taking the chance we might be seen but knowing the pathetic moonlight and Kyle's penlight wouldn't be enough for the killer headline shots I needed.

flash

The tower's surface was corroded like the texture of coral. It was a brilliant crimson, wet and glistening.

flash

Another close-up of the surface highlighting the tiny pockmarks, the veiny texture, the smooth bulbous tumours, and small red branches that spiked up out of the main tower. White, fibrous bulbs hung heavy at the tips of every branch.

flash

The eldritch spike was all sharp edges, strange angles, and deep holes with living darkness. Its very material was twisted up similar to the fibres of a muscle.

flash

This shot was beautiful. An upwards perspective highlighting the pinnacle piercing the very moon itself, creating a dizzying view that almost made one sick to look at. Backlit by the moonlight, the looming alien spire was awful.

I lowered my camera to my chest.

"What – what is that thing? It looks like a plant," Kyle whispered.

"I don't know but whatever it is, it's huge. It's not moving with the current at all, so it must be anchored to the ocean floor," I replied, trying to imagine the immensity and failing.

"The meteor that broke apart in the atmosphere, do you think the chunks of stone contained seeds of some kind?" Kyle asked. "Seeds that rooted in the ocean floor and sprouted this thing?"

"It explains why the government is so keen on hiding it. The meteor fragment landed, what, only a week ago? This thing grew this tall in only a week? They are likely trying to quarantine it. Good luck with that considering it's planted in the ocean and could be spreading who knows where on the currents."

A chilling wind picked up. The ocean surface was no longer calm. As it became choppier, sharp waves slapped at me, pushing me towards the obelisk. I paddled back a bit, to put some distance between it and me.

"It has to be some kind of extraterrestrial plant," Kyle said, struggling against the waves.

"Does it look fleshy to you? Like the skin on the inside of your mouth or something? It reminds me of mucous membrane."

"That's disturbing and I honestly didn't need that imagery. Got all the pictures you need? We need to get ashore before daybreak."

"Hold on, I want a couple more shots," I said.

I ignored his sigh, putting my eye to my viewfinder, and taking another half dozen photos. As I finally dropped my camera to my chest, we were hit by the biggest wave yet. My surfboard tilted to the left, I felt the icy water engulf my knee, and I panicked. Crying out, I reached blindly with my hand to catch myself. My palm hit the surface of the obelisk, sinking into its spongy flesh. Reflexively, I dug my nails in while I pulled myself upright.

"Fuck, Marnie, let's get out of here!" Kyle said.

It happened in a moment – one frozen in time like a photograph – I opened my mouth to reply as my mind registered that my hand had sunk up to my wrist in the meaty surface. Pain shot up my arm as my hand and wrist were crushed by something inside the pinnacle.

"Get it off! Oh God, Kyle, help me!" I squealed.

His jaw hung as he stared at where my arm ended and the alien flesh began.

"Kyle!" My voice rose in a terrorized shriek.

He snapped out of it and, grabbing my leg to pull himself up to me, braced a foot against the tower. He gripped my arm and pulled. The pressure responded by tightening down on my hand, grinding from side to side. It felt like my skin was being flayed off my arm and I nearly bit through my lip preventing a scream from boiling over.

Kyle's muscles bulged under his wet suit as he strained. Abruptly my arm pulled free, trailing thin, goopy ropes of alien mucus. Kyle and I fell back against our boards and, as one, took up our paddles and desperately fled back to shore. The waves helped us, pushing us up and forward on the swells. Without them, I would never have made it. My arm was on fire, my left hand was weak and barely able to grasp the paddle. I was afraid of the moment that I would see it in the light, see what damage had been done.

We sped by unseen by the ships and their sweeping lights. I almost cried out in relief when I felt the numbed soles of my feet drag across sand. Kyle jumped off his surfboard, splashing to my side. He wrapped an arm around my waist, pulling me from my board and farther onto the beach.

"Let me see your arm." Kyle fumbled his cellphone out of the duffel bag he'd left on the sand, activating the light function.

I held my arm out, I couldn't stop trembling.

"Oh fuck, you're okay, you're fine!"

Kyle fell back on his ass, laughing. Unbelieving, I snatched the phone and shone it on my left arm. My skin was unblemished, unmarked, whole. The pain had subsided into a dull ache interrupted occasionally by an irritating stinging.

"It felt like teeth," I said, clenching and unclenching my hand. "It was like a set of giant teeth had clamped down on my arm."

"Teeth?"

Kyle wasn't looking at me. He was looking everywhere but me, throwing all the gear into his jeep and mounting the boards to the rack on the roof. His voice quavered. Finished with packing, he stood with his back to the ocean, bouncing his keys on his palm.

"It bit me, Kyle, the teeth – they were massive, like the size of watermelons!"

"Get in the Jeep, Marnie," Kyle snapped. "Let's get out of here. You've got your pictures, you've got everything you need, so let's go."

He was afraid, I could hear it in his voice. I struggled to my feet, my legs afire with returning circulation, and limped after him. In the car, as Kyle pulled away with his headlights off, I massaged my wrist. Kyle turned off the beach road onto the ramp to the highway, he flicked on the Jeep's headlights, and I heard him breathe a sigh of relief.

"This is going to make one hell of a story, Marnie," he said, glancing over at me.

Despite my heart only having just slowed to a normal pace, I snorted with laughter.

"I promise I'll remember you when I win a Pulitzer!" I said.

For an insane minute we both laughed, then we lapsed into an uneasy silence. A half hour later, we pulled into the parking lot of my motel. Kyle parked and left his Jeep idling.

"Do you want to come up? For a drink maybe?" I asked.

"I can't, Marnie. You know I can't."

My face flushed.

"I didn't mean like that –"

"My wife's waiting for me." He reached across the center console and gripped my left hand in his right. "But this meant a lot to me, seeing you, spending time with you. I'm glad we did this, and if I weren't married…"

I pulled my hand from his. The skin had begun tingling again. I grabbed my stuff and got out, not turning back when he called my name. I slammed the car door against his voice and escaped to my motel room. I hoped he'd knock. I hated myself for wanting that, for wanting to feel like I was more desirable than his wife, that I was more important.

Carmen was waiting for me as I came down the escalator from the arrivals area. She'd taken the day off work to meet me, even though I told her I could grab an Uber. She had a bouquet of daisies in one hand, an iced mocha in the other – my favourites. I smiled and my heart felt like bursting as I hugged her tight against me. She laughed in my ear, warning me to be careful of the drink. I grabbed her beautiful face, feeling her umber skin beneath my palm as soft as silk, and kissed her full on the lips.

When we got home, we fell into bed for a blissful afternoon. The sunlight dwindled to soft evening ambiance as we lay naked together. I inhaled the soft scent of lavender from her black curls and tried to ignore the painful tingling in my left arm that hadn't stopped since yesterday.

She stirred, got up on her elbows, and stared at my face, examining it. I held my breath, waited, hoped the guilt wouldn't show.

"I wish I didn't have to ask, but did you meet up with him?" she asked.

"Carmen, please," I started but she shook her head.

"I want to trust you, trust that you kept your promise to me, but I need to hear it from you."

"I didn't break my promise, Carmen, I didn't meet up with Kyle, okay?"

She smiled and relaxed. She fell asleep soon after, her legs wrapped around mine, her head on my shoulder, her hand cupping my breast.

I felt like I was suffocating. Trapped in her embrace, caught in my own guilt. I didn't cheat on her again, but I would have if Kyle had followed me up to my room. I was such a pathetic asshole. If I cared about Carmen, I would tell her the truth, let her leave me so she could find someone deserving of her.

But I knew I wouldn't.

I was a coward.

I woke up with a gasp. The pain in my left hand was burning its way up my arm and into my left shoulder. I sat up, my breath hissing furiously through my clenched teeth. Carmen had left for work already, I was alone.

I stumbled my way to the bathroom and turned on the

powerful vanity lights. My hand felt as though it should be twice its size, swollen and bruised. It wasn't. In fact, my left hand looked smaller than my right. The skin was painfully dry, cracking across the palm, through the knuckles, and around the nailbeds.

My whole hand was an angry red with the skin beneath my nails a vivid crimson. Strawberry streaks crept up my arm before trailing off at the base of my shoulder. Pulling my fingers into a fist took more effort than was normal, I could feel the skin tightening. The cracks deepened and bled. I turned on the faucet, blasting my hand with ice cold water.

My mind pulled me back to the night on the ocean and I shuddered at the vivid memory of my hand plunging into the alien plant, the feeling of being pinned in place by the bite of some behemoth horror's teeth.

I retched. Clinging to the sink with my good hand, I tried to keep my left under the water as I gagged. Having not eaten anything for hours, only ropes of bile dribbled out of my mouth, souring it and making me gag harder.

Fumbling a bottle of ibuprofen from the cabinet behind the mirror, I swallowed three with water gulped from the faucet. I stayed there until the pain subsided some thirty minutes later.

I examined my hand. The skin was still taut and red. I got out the antiseptic cream, slathering most of the tube onto my skin, and then wrapped my hand in a towel to keep the moisture in. To be safe, I popped an antihistamine in case it was some kind of severe allergic reaction.

Going to my desk, I logged into my laptop. Emails from my editor waited for me. Typing with one hand, I let him know that my article was forthcoming with fantastic pictures to accompany it. I didn't know if that last part was true. My heart pounding, I forgot about the pain for a moment as I pulled my camera from my backpack. I uploaded all the pictures to my computer and began opening them.

The feeling of success was intense – the sight of these vivid, monstrous scenes was life-changing. The images were ominous and shadowy. The pillar was pocked with shadowed recesses, dark flesh constricted over unseen bones. The monster was revealed in all its bright and crimson glory, glistening and bulging with life.

I felt hot all over despite the central air on full blast. My skin pimpled up as my hair rose and my left hand throbbed in time with my heartbeat. These photos were unforgettable, unbelievable, they were out of this world. These photos were going to send my career into the stratosphere. I licked my lips.

My heart racing, I poured myself a gin and tonic to celebrate. The painkillers kicked in, the alcohol kicked in, and I lost myself in the work.

I came to myself as I attached the photos and article to an email. I sent it to my editor, feeling immense satisfaction in hearing the mouse click on the send button. I glanced at the tiny clock in the bottom right-hand corner of my computer screen, it was past four. Buzzed on the gin I'd been drinking all day, I looked down at my arm in numb detachment.

My flesh was covered in angry bumps, close in appearance to headless pimples. This minefield of painful cysts had climbed its way up my forearm, my upper arm, and across my shoulder and chest. My skin was dry, so dry that flexing my fingers caused fresh blood to well up in the fissures.

I grimaced. Just trying to move my wrist was difficult. The hardened skin around my shoulder and chest ached when I breathed in and it was a struggle to raise my arm at all.

I heard the apartment door unlock and open. Carmen was home. I stood, shoving my chair back, and I dashed to the bathroom, slamming and locking the door behind me.

She called out to me. I stared at my arm. Whatever rash or infection I'd gotten from the alien coral was hideous. There was no way I would be able to hide it from Carmen.

"Marnie?"

I slathered more cream over my arm. The motion of rubbing it in set my skin on fire. I bit my lip, trying not to cry. Carmen knocked at the door.

"Can you hand me the ibuprofen?" she asked.

I unlocked the door, tucking my arm behind me and shoving the bottle out between the small crack I made between the door and the frame. Shutting the door again, I heard her shake some pills out, walking away. In my pocket, my phone rang. I pulled it out. It was Kyle. Feeling guilty again, I stepped into the tub and I pulled the curtain closed to create another barrier between me and Carmen.

"Kyle?" I whispered, cupping my hand around my mouth and the phone.

"Fuck, Marnie, is anything happening to your hand? Is – are you sick?"

I felt cold all over. I realized I was using my left hand to cup my phone close to my face. I became hyper aware of the coarse, dry skin of my palm brushing against my lips. Were my lips starting to burn now? Was it like HPV, spread by simple skin contact?"

"Kyle, what are you talking about?"

First instinct – deny. If this was some sort of alien virus, the government would get involved, there'd be quarantine procedures, maybe even experimentation. I'd disappear and never come back.

"My kids are sick, they have fevers. The baby, oh fuck, I picked him up when I got home, he had been crying. The skin on the back of his head, it's all red and dry now, just like my right hand." He was hyperventilating now.

"Kyle, calm down. Babies get all sorts of weird rashes." I chewed bottom lip, trying to think of what to say.

"I grabbed your hand, remember? Before you went up to your hotel room, I held your hand and now –"

Was that a clicking on the line? Some kind of static? Could someone be listening in? My heart was pounding in my chest.

"Kyle, we can't talk about this. We can't know if someone is listening in," I said.

"Who gives a shit if someone is listening? What are we supposed to do? I have to take them to the hospital, it's spreading. I have to tell them what we did, what we saw –"

"Kyle, don't. They, the government, they'll take your kids away. They'll keep them like lab rats and arrest us both. I'm hanging up now. I have to go, don't call again. They're listening." I ended the call over his shouting.

He called back right away and I silenced it. He called again and again. I turned my phone off.

I got out of the tub. My big hot-pink robe hung on the hook on the back of the door. I pulled it on, tying it tight around my waist. The sleeves were wide and long, hanging down past my very fingertips. Usually I rolled the sleeves up for convenience's sake, not this time.

Carmen was making dinner. I made my way into our tiny kitchen and leaned against the counter. Her face was flushed, her brow sweaty.

"Are you okay?" My stomach was sinking to my feet.

She turned to me with a bright smile. "I'm fine, just a headache really. A pack of seven-year-olds will do that to you. At that age, all they do is scream and shout."

I felt lightheaded with relief. Kyle was wrong. His kid just had a baby rash of some kind. He was overreacting and I was just having an allergic reaction. It made sense, why wouldn't I have an allergic reaction to touching some alien plant?

"Hungry?" Carmen asked.

I went to sleep in my robe and woke up in agony. The whole left side of my upper body was scorched and wave after wave of painful prickles rushed through my skin. It was the very same pins-and-needles feeling I would get after a leg or arm fell asleep. It was pure torture.

Whimpering under my breath, I pulled my robe open. The redness had stretched down, past my hip and halfway down my left thigh. I twisted my body, so my legs were hanging off the edge of the bed. I slid off, onto my feet and, using the nightstand for support, pulled myself into a standing position. My phone was on the nightstand, still turned off. I powered it up again with my right hand.

My left hand, I noticed with a kind of frozen detachment, wouldn't flex at all. My fingers were petrified in a crimson carapace. I lifted my left arm higher, into the light filtering through the window. The skin across my chest tightened and the cysts that covered my left breast popped with soft squelches. Pinkish pus dripped across my belly as bright, shocking knives of pain ripped through my body. The viscous chunky ichor reeked of decay, of rot.

I dropped my arm to my side, crying out. Panicking, I hobbled to the bathroom, turning the shower on. Stepping under the boiling water, I gritted my teeth against the pain as I scrubbed soap over my chest and shoulder with my one good hand. My open sores began to bleed but I took that as a good sign, anything better than the foul-smelling pus.

When the hot water had run out, I stepped out onto the bathmat. Facing the mirror over the sink, I examined myself. The hot water had turned all my uninfected skin beet-red to match the rest. I turned around, trying to see the extent of the infection, when I saw Carmen behind me.

She was clutching the bathroom door frame, her eyes feverish. On her face and her neck, I could see the tell-tale crimson stain. I remembered the night I came back, I remembered falling into her arms, the alien structure forgotten for that sweet afternoon.

"What the hell is wrong with your skin?" Carmen asked, her voice quavering.

"It's just a rash," I lied.

She pulled up her shirt. The skin around her hips was painted with an intense cherry splash. I didn't want to know how much farther down it went, I didn't need to see it, a part of me already knew.

"I had to leave work early, I thought maybe what I was coming down with was contagious. I guess it is," she said, letting her shirt drop and clenching her fists. "What did you do, Marnie? What did you give me?"

"It's just an allergic reaction because I touched it, it's just a rash!" I was shouting, why was I shouting?

"Touched what, Marnie? Touched *what*?!"

"That alien thing that I went to photograph! Kyle and I – we paddled out to it and I got knocked into it and I touched it. That's all it is, an allergic reaction. I couldn't go to the doctor, I couldn't say anything, they're watching, and they're listening in on my phone calls, when Kyle called, they were listening, and –" I forced my mouth to shut, sucking in air through my nose.

"Kyle."

She stared at me. In the bedroom, my phone started to ring.

"How am I supposed to trust you, Marnie?"

The voicemail kicked in. It began to ring again.

"Nothing happened between us, he was just helping me."

She was crazy. She was freaking out that I met up with an old friend and didn't care at all that I'd broken the story of the century, of all the centuries.

"You lied to me and now you've infected us both with some kind of sickness, you lied to me, you fucking lied!"

I tried to cross my arms, remembered my left was non-functional, and settled for putting my right hand on my hip. In the bedroom, my phone rang and rang.

"I understand you're upset but this is my big break, this

is it. My editor is going to be publishing the story and after that, I'm set – we're set!"

"I work with children, Marnie! Children!"

She turned from me, storming into the bedroom where my phone rang still. I wanted to chase after her, but the best I could do was stumble to door frame and fall against it.

"Carmen, please!" I shouted.

She came out with purse in hand.

"I am going to the ER. I suggest you do the same. After that, I expect to find you gone," she said, snarling, crazed.

"I did this for us, Carmen! Listen to me!"

"You didn't, you *didn't*! You did this for yourself!" she spat. "You can take your story and shove it up your ass!"

Then she was gone, slamming the front door behind her. I hung onto the door jamb, waiting, hoping she'd change her mind and come back. After a while I gave up and limped into the bedroom. My phone was where I left it. Eleven missed calls, ten new messages. Most were from Kyle, begging me to call him, demanding that I answer, crazed texts filled with profanities and typos. A couple were from my editor. He wasn't going to be publishing my story. He didn't believe it was real. He questioned my integrity if I was willing to go to such lengths to cause a scandal and panic by photoshopping something so absurd.

Of course he was lying. You'd have to be blind to think the photos had been faked. The government had gotten involved. If they were tapping my phone, it would be just as easy for them to monitor my outgoing emails.

In my hand, my phone started ringing again. I didn't look at the caller ID. It didn't matter who it was, they'd be listening. Instead, I threw my phone against the wall and watched it shatter. Of course, I had to wonder, why hadn't they come to get me yet?

As the adrenaline died down and I stared at my destroyed phone, my mind settled. I had to get back into control, I felt like I was losing it. I returned to the bathroom, shedding my robe as I went. I used the last of the antibacterial cream over as much of my body as I could. Then I topped all that with my creamiest lotion, hoping that the extra hydration would help.

Naked, I made my way to the living room. Laying on the couch, I turned the TV on in hopes that it would help distract me. Sinking into the cushions, feeling my skin burn and prickle, I cried. Carmen was right, I should have told her right when I got home. I should have gone to the hospital. I imagined her going to work and tousling a kid's head, helping another tie their shoes, hugging a third. She could have infected the whole class.

I had to make it up to her. I had to make things right. Carmen would be back after getting some antibiotics from the doctor and then we would talk. She'd bring me to the hospital and we'd both get better. We'd get past this.

I let my eyes focus on the TV screen, where a spray-tanned hunk of a news anchor stood in front of a green screen as it played and re-played the same shoddy camera footage.

"Authorities are advising all to stay in their homes, shut off your air conditioning, and seal the windows and doors as best you can."

Behind him was the eldritch alien spire, backlit by

an afternoon sun. It had changed since I'd last seen it, its surface was now spotted with huge alabaster blossoms. As the footage continued, one burst and thousands upon thousands of pale seeds exploded up and outwards.

"They refuse to comment on what exactly this strange infection is, except that it is extremely contagious and is spread by touch. If you see one of these seeds, do not try to destroy it yourself. Please call your local police department right away. And again, do not leave your homes. If you are at a hospital or school, please remain there until the police have issued otherwise."

Behind him, the camera shook and the tower grew smaller as the person who was filming fled from it. More blossoms burst until the very sun was obscured by the seedlings that floated weightlessly on the wind towards shore. Then the film was jarred, images flickered by, until it settled on a shot of the seed-choked sky and was cut.

The image changed to the news anchor interviewing someone else on the ramifications this had on our idea of extraterrestrial life.

I tried to get up, but my waist was locked. Breathing was a conscious effort. I tried to look down but couldn't. I ran my right hand under the robe, feeling my body. A fissured crust caked my left shoulder and the entirety of my chest. The skin was rough. It felt like a layer of thick salt had dried on me. While I felt like I was burning up with a fever, the areas infected were cool to the touch – they felt inanimate, something apart from me. Running my fingers over it created a harsh rasping sound.

My probing fingers found that my breasts were

constricted to half their normal size and were rock-hard. The rash had gone on to infect most of my belly and hips, as well. I knocked on the shell over my belly button and, though I heard the impact of my knuckles on the skin, couldn't feel a thing. It had spread lower, but my courage fled, and I couldn't bring myself to explore what had happened below my waist. I couldn't feel my left leg and when I tried to flex my right, it would only tremble on the cushions. I was trapped.

The news had moved on to the section normally reserved for weather. Now the weather man illustrated the predicted path, based on wind patterns, of the toxic seedlings spreading across the nation. It was late, but I knew Carmen would come back for me. She wouldn't leave me here, knowing what bad shape I was in. I settled my head back into the cushions and tried to make myself as comfortable as possible. Carmen would come back for me.

On the screen, the news anchor re-stated the warning to stay inside, to seal up windows and doors, to stay safe. Feeling exhausted, I let my eyelids slip shut. As I sunk into the black comfort of sleep, I smiled. In the morning, Carmen would be back to get me, and everything would be fixed.

Was it morning? I couldn't open my eyes. Panic mounted. My chest was constricted. My mouth was sealed shut. Only the barest whisper of air whistled through my thickened nostrils. That was what had woken me. The feeling of suffocation. My ears were deafened, trapping me in a deprivation chamber.

Where was Carmen? She had abandoned me. Everyone had abandoned me. My body was trapped in a crimson carapace and I was burning up with an infernal heat. My whole being was melting in the scorching hell that was my own body.

One last ditch effort. I strained. The pain was incredible, white-hot needles stabbing my face. My right eyelid shuddered. I caught the hint of light. I forced it more, using all my willpower. My eyelid felt like carpenter nails dragging over my eyeball, but I got it open.

There I was, still laid out on the couch. Warm midmorning sunlight leaked in, revealing my body, which now served as my sarcophagus.

At some point in the night, my robe had slipped open. I could just see the length of my body in my narrow field of vision. Horror mounted as I gazed upon it. My arms had curled up against my chest by the ever-tightening pull of the rash. My legs were fused together, feet misshapen and crushed.

As it tightened, the alien rash had also blossomed out in large white flowers all over my belly, my thighs, my breasts.

It was beautiful. I was a garden. It was terrible. I had been made into a deliverer of death. Upon each flower, thousands of feathery seedlings stirred with each weakened breath. At any moment they would unlatch and fill the apartment with poisonous death.

I closed my eye. It was getting harder and harder to breathe. I counted my breaths until I could take them no more

The Whale Hunts

Henry leaned over the side of the powerful yacht and stared down at the inky waters of the midnight sea. Behind him, Louie and Elena were checking the harpoon chest in the middle of the ship, repacking the harpoons so that they would be easy to grab. Henry could see the receding light of the city of New York II.

He looked back at the thick black waters. Henry reckoned that they were above the sunken city of New York I, lost in the cataclysm of 2071. Elena came up to his side. She would have been beautiful if her face hadn't been disfigured by the acid her husband had thrown at her after she fled their marriage with their young daughter.

"Anything?" she asked.

"We wouldn't see it even if it was down there. No one's

seen it properly, the water is too dark," he said.

Elena shrugged and smiled. The smile made her mass of scar tissue scrunch up in thick wrinkles. Henry wondered if it hurt her to smile.

"Nothing on radar," Captain Richardson called from the helm.

No one knew the Captain's real name. When he'd first met the convicts, he'd refused to shake their hands or introduce himself. He just sucked on his pipe and looked them all up and down before nodding and letting them pass him on their way onto his ship. Elena started calling him Captain Richardson and everyone else followed suit, he never bothered to correct them.

He wasn't one of them. He was rich, bored, and desperate for something to make his life more interesting. The fading ring of lighter skin on his left ring finger marked him as a widower or divorcee. Henry assumed that the Captain liked the excitement and danger of the Hunt, of being one of the few free men allowed to sail the Black Sea. Henry had never bothered to ask the Captain if this was true, he knew the old man would never answer.

"Are we above New York, Captain?" he asked instead.

The gray old man scratched at the white whiskers on his chin and snorted around his pipe.

"Above New York, you say? I'd say we left the sorry sunken bitch a mile back. We're in the proper Atlantic now, son!"

The heavy British accent he had was questionable since it tended to fade when the Captain was distracted.

"Captain, harpoons are set," Louie shouted.

Henry shivered a bit in the cold wind that picked up

off the dark water. It smelled sour and rotten. He zipped up his windbreaker and looked out over the water. He'd been on over two dozen Hunts, a dozen trips for every murder, but each time felt as terrifying as the last. Most criminals managed to survive their sentences without a single sighting or encounter of The Whale. Of course, those that did encounter It simply disappeared, boat and all.

Louie, Elena, and Henry joined the Captain at the helm. The Captain pulled a gold cross from under his thin button-up and held it out so it dangled in his fist at the end of a thick gold chain.

One by one, the three convicts placed their left hands on top of his fist.

"Lend us your strength, O Lord, so that we four might slay the great Leviathan that struck so deadly a blow to our hallowed nation. Guide us through this dark night, over the Black Sea, and into the dawn. Guide our spears true. And if it is Your plan, O Lord, to sink us low, let us each die with glory and courage in our hearts," the Captain intoned.

"Amen," said the rest, obediently.

The Captain nodded and tucked his cross away. The three convicts descended back onto the main deck and took their positions. Elena was at the starboard harpoon gun, Louie at the port, and Henry at the gun bolted to the very front of the ship. Henry looked over his shoulder.

Fierce, crazed Louie was grinning. He'd be sailing the Hunt until the day he died of old age after shooting up his high school graduation ceremony. His shaven head gleamed in the light of the thin sickle moon and was crowned with a blotchy tattoo of twin snakes entwined and spitting red venom.

Elena had tied back her thick curly brown hair with a rubber band. Her marred face was serene and calm. This was to be her last Hunt. She had been lucky, she had only managed to put her husband into intensive care after she'd tried to kill him with a hammer. For aggravated assault, convicts only had to serve an abbreviated sentence on the Black Sea.

The Captain looked as relaxed as he always did on the water. The thin moon was hanging above his head like an Egyptian halo. His tarry teeth were out in full view as he clenched his old pipe between them, his faded blue sailor's hat tilted back on his balding head at a jaunty angle. Henry wondered, not for the first time, how much of the Captain's persona was affected to emulate an ideal of the stereotypical swarthy pirate captain of old.

"Keep your eyes on the Sea, son!" the Captain shouted at him.

Henry nodded and blushed a bit when he caught Elena looking his way. He settled back in his hard plastic lawn chair and peered out over the water for any signs of movement. The Black Sea was as dead as ever, void of even a ripple or wave. Henry leaned over the salt-eaten railing. Reaching out, he dipped his fingers into the icy waters.

The Atlantic Ocean used to be all blues and greens and grays, but never black. That had all changed the day of the cataclysm. The whole Eastern coast of the United States and Canada had been hit by a massive earthquake. The violence of the tremors had been off the charts.

The cataclysm happened overnight, no warning, no chance to escape so tons of thousands of people had died when the cities had come crashing down around their heads. New York, Rhode Island, Newfoundland, New Brunswick, and Florida had all been lost. Whole cities had been swallowed by the earth and waves. Rising from the ocean, tsunamis had appeared as roaring giants, pounding the remaining coastlines as thousands of people fled inland. After a day of terror, the waves calmed and only the aftershocks remained.

That and the dark stain that appeared off the coastline, a mile from where New York City used to be. Scientists from all around the world guessed that this was where the earthquake had originated so the government sent a team to investigate.

All seven of the divers disappeared. The only record left was one of the underwater cameras that had resurfaced, miles away and caught by a net.

The footage showed the divers descending into the indigo depths and towards the mysterious inky blob that clung to the ocean floor. The divers spread out, aimed their flashlights into the darkness, and swam into it. The camera's view darkens. And that's it.

"Eyes on the Sea, Henry, unless you want to end up as Whale food," the Captain shouted over the sound of the engine.

Henry jerked his hand out of the water and shook his head. He hadn't realized that he had tuned out. He sat back in his seat. The yacht sliced through the thick waters, spraying the air with salty droplets. The mist freckled Henry's face as he peered into the night. Out of reflex, he licked his lips and immediately regretted it.

The water tasted foul. Gone was the clean and bitter taste of salt and seaweed. After the dark stain had appeared, all the marine life had died and as the ocean had died, the stain grew larger and larger. The water tasted of feces, old coffee grounds, and rotting fruit. It smelled even worse, hot and musky and overpowering.

After three years, the whole eastern coast was changed from the shoreline to over forty miles out. The Black Sea showed no signs of slowing its growth and the foul water stretched farther and farther.

The fishing industry died with the ocean. Of course, people began to claim sightings of The Whale hunting. They blamed it for eating all the fish. Henry had heard all the theories. The Whale was an ancient apex predator stirred up out of the depths after the cataclysm, or that it was a giant squid drawn up due to over-fishing, or a long-necked dinosaur enraged by the oil drilling. Whatever it was, Henry was confident that the heavy steel harpoons they had would pierce Its damned hide.

The night was quiet. The Captain took them right up to where the black waters ended and the clean, blue ocean began. He cut off the engine so they could all have something to eat and drink before making the long journey back. Henry looked down at the two bodies of water that met so calmly together. The border between was perfectly straight and even.

Elena called to him and he joined her and Louie. The three convicts sat in a loose ring by Elena's harpoon gun. Elena always brought something home cooked, spicy, and fragrant. This night, it was a simple chickpea and carrot curry on jasmine rice. Henry had brought some ham and cheese sandwiches. Crazy Louie always brought the same thing, a small jar of sweet pickles.

Captain Richardson never ate anything with them. Whether it was because he thought himself above them or because he wanted to keep an eye on the ocean at all times, Henry didn't know. The Captain also refused to eat any of their food and he never brought any of his own. Every night, he would lean back against the railing, stare up at the sky, and smoke his pipe.

Louie had already cracked open his jar of pickles and was taking a deep swallow of the yellow brine. Elena had waited for Henry before bowing her head in prayer. Henry closed his eyes and waited for her to finish.

The first time Elena had done this, he'd felt uncomfortable and out of place. If there was a God, he obviously didn't care enough to stop The Whale from slowly killing the ocean and starving the United States. Over a few days, Henry got used to it. She never asked him to pray along with her or for Louie to refrain from eating until she was done. So, Henry closed his eyes and listened.

The Captain always set his anchor down so that his yacht sat half in the ocean and half in the Black Sea. The waves from each had its own sound. The ocean sounded soft, light, and gentle. The waves of the Black Sea were harsher, thicker, and sucked at the side of the ship in greedy slurps.

"Amen," Elena said and opened the big thermos of curry.

She poured the steaming food onto the bowls of rice she'd already prepared. Henry passed out a sandwich to everyone. Louie didn't offer anyone a pickle.

"Why do you drink the brine?" Henry asked, finally, after weeks of wondering.

The wild-eyed young man shrugged one shoulder.

"Maybe if I drunk enough, I'll become pickled," Louie said.

"What?" Henry said.

"Whale don't want no pickle, It'll be wanting the fresh food," Louie grinned a rotting smile.

Henry looked over at Elena. She smiled and shrugged in imitation of Louie.

"How's your daughter?" Henry asked, trying to ignore Louie's slurps.

Elena put down her sandwich. She reached into an inside pocket of her bright yellow jacket and pulled out a twice-folded sheet of computer paper. She took great care in unfolding it to reveal a crude crayon drawing featuring bright colours. The drawing was of a woman and a little girl. Henry took it and looked at it a moment. He couldn't remember what it was like to be a kid.

"Very cute," he said, handing it back.

"The probation officer was there the whole time, but we still had fun," Elena said. "He hasn't touched her. I can tell. She finally looks happy."

Elena's smile was sweet but also strained with a subtle sorrow.

"And you, Henry? How are you?"

Henry made a Louie shrug.

"The dating game's been sparse, being a criminal and all. I am afraid the Black Sea smell doesn't help either."

Louie giggled.

"Time to head back," the Captain called.

139

The three convicts packed away their leftovers and returned to their posts. The Captain turned the engine on full, the yacht cut through the water and the Captain aimed her back home.

Henry looked for the moon's reflection in the surface of the Black Sea but couldn't find it. It didn't reflect any kind of light. It was just a monotone, smooth black. He'd never noticed that before, how the reflections were missing. He looked up at the moon hanging over the western horizon like a waiting bone sickle.

The yacht shuddered to a stop. Henry was pitched forward. Only by grabbing the harpoon gun was he able to prevent himself from going overboard. Pushing himself back off the gun, he turned around. Elena was sprawled on her belly on the deck. Louie was gripping the railing with white knuckles. The Captain was gone.

The yacht's engine was still growling, the water frothing behind it as its blades kicked up waves, but the ship wasn't moving forward. It was bucking from side to side, but otherwise remained in the same place. Henry spread his legs for better balance and cupped his hands around his mouth.

"Captain?" he called.

"I think he fell overboard," Elena was getting to her feet.

"Whale got him," Louie said.

Henry took a few steps towards the man, his heart kicked up into his throat.

"You saw him get taken? You saw The Whale?" he asked.

The man shook his shaven head, pressed a finger against the side of his nose and snorted phlegm into the water.

"Didn't see It. I smelt It," he said.

"What do you mean, you smelled the damned Whale?" Henry's voice pitched high in his fear.

"It smelt like fresh blood."

The two men stared at each other. Henry looked away first, the other man's eyes wild and blank. Keeping his gaze on the slippery deck, Henry joined Elena at the helm. She was turning the wheel, fiddling with the throttle.

"It won't move. It's like it's stuck," she said.

"The anchor – maybe the Captain forgot to bring it back up?" Henry countered.

Louie giggled, drawing their eyes to him as he pointed down at the anchor at the aft side of the yacht. Henry felt his palms begin to tingle, something that always happened when he knew things were about to take a turn for the worst. His palms had tingled when he had seen on the evening news, two months ago, that the plant he worked at had exploded, killing sixty-three people and injuring dozens more.

His palms had tingled when he heard that the investigators had found signs of negligence. That's how Henry had known it was his fault. He'd been the night foreman the shift before the explosion. He'd been the one to sign off on the checklist. He'd been the one to miss the engineer's note about the leaking valve and the request to replace it.

His palms had tingled in the courtroom and Henry had known the judge would declare him guilty on all counts. The next day, he was assigned a place in The Whale Hunters' Lodge, a maximum-security prison just outside the city. A week for every man killed. Sixty-three weeks, thirteen months in total. Now his palms were tingling again.

"Can you get this boat moving, Elena?" he asked.

The woman shook her head.

"It has to be caught on something. A reef?"

"Not possible. All the reefs died with the fish and the goddamn seaweed."

The yacht shook violently and heaved up out of the water before splashing back down.

"Get to your harpoon stations!" Henry barked.

He scrambled over the wet deck, flinging himself onto his gun. A small patch of water on the starboard side burst up as a thick black tentacle rose into the air. The water ran thickly down its length. It stretched fifteen feet high, waving. Henry jerked his harpoon gun to the right, aimed, and squeezed the trigger.

The steel harpoon speared right through the tentacle, shooting out the other side, and landing in the Sea to sink out of sight. Unharmed, the tentacle dropped towards them. Louie screamed as he saw it but didn't have time to dive out of the way. The force of impact splattered him across the deck in gobbets and crimson rain. Henry felt some of Louie's hot blood mist over his face, like the black water had done earlier. He could taste Louie's saltiness and wondered, for a brief insane moment, if he could taste pickles.

Elena was screaming, her hands turning her gun to aim true. Henry heard her harpoon launch. The Sea bulged all around them. Six more giant tentacles breached the surface to weave through the air. They were surrounded. Elena struggled to reload her weapon. He watched her aim and fire. He stood frozen. The yacht was listing to port, Elena's harpoon went wild as everything began to slide. The ship was rising as something was ascending to the surface directly beneath it. Henry fell against the railings, clutched at the corroded metal, and looked over the side at the behemoth under the water.

It was massive. Bigger than any whale he'd ever seen. The yacht tilted farther, began to spin as it slid off the giant's back. The yacht's nose plunged into the Sea, its deck was flooded by the foul water before it broke free and righted itself. Elena was screaming again. Henry turned and saw the woman had been swept under the railings. Her legs dangled off the side of the boat.

He went to her, his feet slipping in the water and the blood. On the starboard side, the black goliath rose higher and higher out of the water. There was a meaty pop as a great black eye appeared in the dark flesh.

Henry fell to his knees and grabbed Elena's outstretched hand. Her body lay over the side of the yacht, between the deck and underneath the railing. He could hear her tiny feet beating a furious tempo against the side of the ship, her other hand gripped the vertical support pole of the railing. He braced his feet and pulled.

He felt her weight ease, begin to rise. Elena's screams intensified. She beat at his hands with her free one, her nails scrambling at his fingers. He reached down and hooked a hand in her armpit for more leverage.

"Let go!" she screamed.

Henry looked down at her upturned, terrified face. He looked up. A tentacle was wrapped around her legs and was pulling her legs upwards. He saw her back bending the wrong way, trapped between him, The Whale, and the railing.

It was too late. He heard the heavy snap as her spine

broke. Her hand went limp in his. He loosened his grip and the tentacle yanked her away, up into the air and then straight down underneath the dark waves. The Whale's vast head sunk out of sight with her.

Henry dove for the harpoon chest. He ignored the harpoons, tossing them onto to the deck to roll all over the place. He pulled out a clunky flare gun. It was already loaded. He took careful aim, leveled the muzzle at the nearest tentacle, and fired.

The super-heated flare struck it dead on and blazed up with an intense burst. Henry could hear the deep sizzle as a thick cloud of steam ascended to the heavens.

The tentacle snapped down beneath the water, dousing the flare and disappearing. The yacht began to tilt again as The Whale's head broke the surface where the tentacle had been. It towered over the ship. Three meaty pops, one after the other, as three eyes opened on the same side. The alien gaze pierced him to his very core. Out of the corner of his own eye, Henry saw the tentacles press and twist together, becoming one enormous appendage.

He didn't want to die. He wasn't a real murderer. It'd been an accident. He didn't deserve this. It had been negligence, not murder – not murder!

Henry was moaning senseless apologies as he fumbled through the harpoon chest, trying to find more flares. He did so blind, unable to tear his gaze away from the terrible stare of The Whale. His palms were tingling, his fingers were numb, but he clutched at a single flare. He loaded it into the gun. The single, huge tentacle had risen high enough to blot out the moon. Henry raised the gun, closed one eye, and fired. Two of those soulless eyes were closer to one another than the third, it was between these that the flare struck and ignited.

If the intense light and heat hurt The Whale in anyway, It never made a sound to indicate such. The two eyes burst. Heavy, hot black ichor doused Henry. The liquid burned his skin, eating away at his clothes and chest. Behind him, he heard the air whistle as the tentacle came down on him. He threw himself overboard as it crashed onto the deck.

The grimy water washed The Whale's eye gore away and eased the burning only slightly. A part of Henry's mind wondered at the strange thick texture of the Black Sea, so different and unnatural compared to the true ocean. In front of him, through the murk, he saw the yacht sinking, cut very nearly in two from the impact. Before his eyes, the ship began to crumple and break apart, in the grip of something he could not make out through the gloom.

Lungs burning, he kicked at the water, trying to reach the surface. At first he met resistance. The Dark Sea was heavy and it weighed on his limbs, pushing, rejecting his survival with vicious intent. Henry had to fight, rather than swim, to the surface. Breaking through at last, Henry sucked in a delicious gasp of air.

Heart pounding, Henry twisted this way and that, searching for the behemoth. The Whale was gone. The Black Sea was still and empty. There wasn't any debris from the yacht even to show where it had been.

He treaded water, his mind frozen as to what he should do. He turned himself around and around in circles. The Sea was sucking at his legs, pulling at his chest. He was getting tired. Henry stopped turning. Ahead of him, he could see the gentle clean waves of the uninfected ocean.

Henry began to swim. The Captain had only gotten them a quarter of a mile away from the border between Sea and ocean before The Whale had caught them. It was a distance that would have been easy to manage except that the dark water was sucking at him, pushing back to try and keep him away from the ocean. Several times, the Black Sea jumped up and plunged into his mouth, choking him. He struggled, his muscles burning with exertion. The dark water rose to meet him, Henry floundered. He couldn't keep his head above the Black Sea. He stopped swimming and treaded the water. He'd lost sight of the ocean, all he could see was a high wave of darkness.

The Black Sea was rising in a thick, slow wall. Henry now knew that The Whale meant to keep him and his palms were screaming with pinpricks. He sucked in a deep breath and plunged beneath the surface. He kicked and clawed and beat at It, pulling himself forward at a snail's pace.

His head buzzed, his heart crashed about in his chest, between his burning lungs. Still he kicked his legs, giving everything he had left. Reaching out with his hands, he prayed to feel the lighter, thinner water of the ocean.

Henry's gaze grew dark, spotted. The Whale began to crush him, squeezing his body as though he was trapped between gelatinous jaws that spanned for miles. Around his legs, he felt something tightening, burning, stinging. He screamed, his air streaming away from his face in tiny bubbles. His hand broke through and he felt cold night air.

He felt despair. The darkness had tricked him and

he'd gotten twisted about. He'd been swimming nowhere, nowhere and upward rather than to safety. Now The Whale would have him. Henry's head broke through. He looked and saw the indigo ocean below him. His mind had a moment to recognize that he was hanging out of The Whale three feet above where the real ocean line was before he fell out of the living wall, plunging face first into the water. Caught by surprise, Henry swallowed a bellyful of the salty water. When he broke surface again, he vomited. With violent groans, he expelled the hot, burning remains of Elena's curry and his cheese sandwiches. Above him, the sickle moon shone on, unchallenged.

Bleary eyed, Henry back-paddled away from his floating island of bile. He kept his back to the open ocean, never taking his eyes away from the Black Sea. His legs were stinging as if they'd been burned.

As he watched, the dark wall of what he now understood was The Whale itself sank back down, stopping just a foot or so above proper sea level. Henry's limbs were heavy with exhaustion, but he forced them to carry him ever backwards, away from the cursed Sea. All along the border between the Sea and the ocean, tentacles rose up. They reached out and swept through the ocean waves, probing. The Whale was looking for him.

When he felt his back hit something hard, he let out a thin scream. He splashed in place, twisting to look over his shoulder. Behind him, an old buoy danced on the shallow waves, its light long dead. His whole body shaking, Henry wrapped his arms around one of the buoy's thick, salt-eaten struts. He looked back the way he'd come.

The tentacle directly in front of him was swirling its tip through his dinner. More tentacles rose out of the depths to join it, first exploring the vomit, then sweeping from side to side in great arcs.

There was no way The Whale could reach him, he half-prayed, half-reasoned. There was no way. The tentacles, finding nothing, expanded their search in wider arcs. Henry held his breath, tried not to move. The tentacles stretched and stretched. His heart burst into a painful palpitation as one swept past mere feet from where the buoy floated. Then the tentacles relaxed into the water and were sucked back into Its endless flank. From afar, Henry watched as the border of black sank back down to sea level and grew still.

To the east, the horizon began to lighten as the sun prepared to rise. The cold waters lapped around Henry's waist in a playful dance. He relished the clean touch, even as his body temperature dropped, and he began to shiver violent spasms.

He tightened his arms around the strut and rested his head against the metal. No one would come for him. All the ships would be turning back with the dawn. The Hunts only happened at night, when The Whale was most active. Henry was stranded, at least until the next night.

"Hen...ry."

He tensed, every muscle sparking. That voice had sounded familiar, but that would be impossible.

"P...lease."

In the pale dawn light, Henry scanned the ocean, but it wasn't true, it couldn't be true. And yet... There she was, struggling in the Black Sea, treading the oily liquid but just barely.

"Elena?"

"Hen…ry…"

Her voice carried over the waves in a faint plea. A violent shiver ripped through Henry's body: part chill, part terror. He looked over his shoulder, scanning the distant horizon as if – by some miracle – help would be coming from the direction of the open sea.

"I… I can't…please," she called to him.

A colder wave of shame rolled over him as memories of sharing meals sparked to life in his mind, as he remembered the face of her daughter in the photo she carried with her always. What kind of person would he be if he didn't even try to save her?

With that new determination flaring as a hot, white flame inside his chest, Henry began to swim toward the edge of the Black Sea. A foot or so from the thickly glistening being, Henry treaded in place and watched. The Whale was stilled, Its massive, miles long, gelatinous body quiet once more. The coming of dawn had put It back to Its daylight slumber.

Henry took a deep, shuddering breath. His body was trembling with the faint remains of adrenaline, fear, and exhaustion; but he thought he could make it. She was only a half dozen feet from him. As he looked to her, he saw her raise a hand towards him, though it quickly dropped below sea level again and she sunk a bit.

"Elena!"

And then he was plunging forward, cutting through the thick viscous entity with strong front strokes and kicking furiously. How sensitive was It? Was It like a spider, instantly aware of when prey touched any part of Its dark web? Would It sense him swimming desperately through Its very body and attack? It didn't matter. In another moment he was there, he was in front of Elena. He reached for her, found only one arm to grip, a smile broke across his face, and then he froze.

The sun had risen higher and now he could see clearly.

Elena was leaning back, her head tilted to the right, and her already scarred face almost fully destroyed by the hungry touch of The Whale. Her eyes had melted partially and stared sightlessly up. Elena's mouth was slack, her lips gone, and still he heard his name being called.

He had to. He had to look.

He could see in the brightening light that her skin was completely eaten away across her chest and shoulders. The arm he couldn't find was actually still there, but it had been reduced to mere bones, loosely connected by stubborn sinew, and which was still attached to her ragged left shoulder, where gristle and muscle was exposed. As he watched, he heard his name again, and as he did, he saw her throat vibrate.

A pressure that felt like a sinuous tongue wrapped around his legs. His shoulders slumped. He gritted his teeth as his body began to tingle, then prickle, then burn. The pain was unbearable. He didn't want to think what was happening to his skin. From the chest down, his body was on fire, his legs were completely without feeling.

In Elena's mouth, he could see clever little appendages coiled in her throat and nestled around her tongue. These dark, eldritch limbs shivered and, as they did, he heard it again.

"Hen...Henry."

He felt a burning in his eyes, this time from tears rather than the acid that was digesting him. The Whale was intelligent. It must have entered through her chest or belly or somewhere else and applied delicate tendrils against her vocal cords in order to mimic her voice.

Henry felt a gentle tug at his waist, playfully pulling him deeper. He reached for Elena and a dark swell rose in response, raising the half-digested, soggy right arm of Elena with it. He had to wonder. Was The Whale mocking him?

The mound cradled her arm as delicately as Elena had likely cradled her daughter so many nights before and The Whale nudged her body closer so Henry could just barely grasp Elena's fingerbones. Weakened by digestive juices, they broke off in his hand with a soft crackle and then The Whale pulled him under.

Henry managed to grab a gasp of air, but he did not struggle. Clutching the fragments of bone in a fist held against his disintegrating chest, Henry tilted his head back and forced his eyes open. In the mere second it took for the destructive black waters to melt his eyes from his sockets, he saw the cheerful rosy glow of ripening daybreak cast a golden hue across the shifting surface of The Whale.

Then he was plunged into darkness and pain

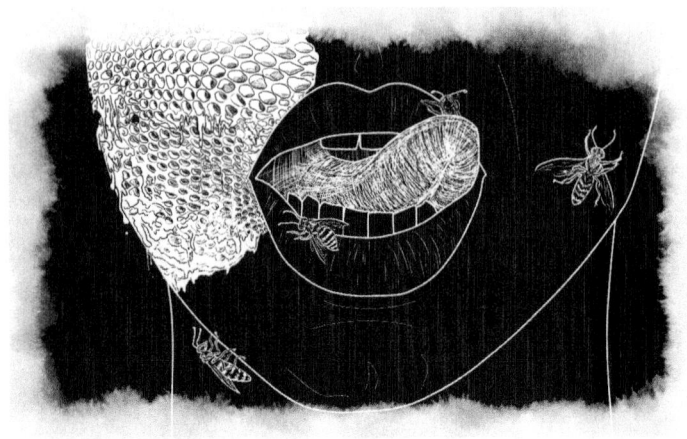

BUZZKILL

The head of an axe makes a strange, slick sound when it slices through the skull of a Hivemind.

The genetic modification was supposed to save the bees, make them more resistant to disease and pests, boost their procreation, and increase their honey production. It did that, and more.

Honey oozes over the axe blade, chunky with what brains remain in the skull of the thing that was once conscious.

Hiveminds used to be people.

All it takes is one moment, one second outside without a suit. The bees are busy little things. It only takes a few seconds for their stings to overwhelm an average sized person, only a few minutes for them to make their way into the skull through the ear canals and set up shop, carving out tunnels and rooms in the soft brain tissue.

With a yank, Anthony pulls the axe free, globs of hot amber liquid land with splats on the grass. He's glad for the suit that protects him from the bees and the smell. Honey from the infesting bees preserves the flesh surrounding the victim's face, allowing it to remain untouched, while the rest of the body slowly decays.

The Hivemind's face droops, the one eye not bursting with honeycombs rolls back into its skull. Bees swarm out of the gaping wound, buzzing with rage as they throw themselves against the man's bulky helmet. Their fuzzy bodies bounce off with dull taps.

Now free of the insects that were keeping it mobile, the body drops to the ground, twitching.

Pulling a grenade from his belt, Anthony pulls the pin, and drops it at his feet. Yellow smoke envelops him and the bees that surround him fall to the ground, their wings fluttering weakly.

Now the hard part. Pesticides don't work on the bees anymore so Anthony grinds each one to smears of ichor with the butt of his axe.

His body aches. This is Anthony's second Hivemind kill of the day. Each infected human can have dozens of bees in their skull and each one has to be stomped out of existence or the bee will rise again, on armoured wings and with an insatiable need to pollinate the soft, gray folds of the flower that makes up a person's mind.

Anthony slips his axe back into its loop on his belt. His arms sing with pain, but his heart finally settles once the adrenaline wears off. Kneeling by the quickly cooling corpse, he lays out a scraper, an oiled leather pouch, and a sharp knife. With these tools, he slices away the skin on the dead man's skull and locates the fat queen. Dropping her on the ground, he then slices her to bits with his knife. After that, he begins to scoop out the rich honey from inside, depositing it into the pouch.

The metal scoop scrapes at the inside of the bony hive until Anthony harvests all the honey. Bits of brain matter pepper the otherwise perfect amber elixir. Finished, Anthony puts away all his tools and sets off at a jog. The sun is setting, it's time for him to go home.

Careful not to get snagged on branches of thorns, Anthony weaves through the trunks until he reaches the edge of the small copse of trees. Before him spreads a magnificent field of grass and wildflowers. At a distance, he spots a Hivemind crouching, on her hands and knees, over a vibrant bunch of cornflowers. In slow, trembling movements, the woman lowers her head down, and rubs her face against the flowers, inhaling all the pollen she can.

Keeping low, Anthony sticks to the edge of the field, making his way east. The Hivemind stands, her face powdered and nostrils flaring. Her mouth drops. Even from where he hides, Anthony can see the squirming insects between her jaws, her cheeks vibrate with their dance. He can hear them buzzing, even over the birdsong.

Shivering, Anthony makes his way past the meadow, down to the river, and across. He's dripping with sweat when he reaches the metal door set into the side of an abandoned house. It leads down to the cellar – the cool, dark place he shares with the love of his life.

She's weeping when he descends the short set of wooden stairs. Her cries hurt his heart. Anthony finds the lantern by the last step and lights it, its buttery illumination painting the stone walls, the dusty wooden shelves, and the few cans of food that remain.

Standing on the thin, dirty mattress in the corner, she strains against the chains on her wrists, desperate to reach the light, drawn to it.

The bees in her mouth rage over her tongue, their facetted eyes catching the faint light like gemstones. He pulls the punch from his belt and opens it, tossing it to the dirt floor by her feet. The cellar is filled with the sound of buzzing hunger.

It takes a moment for her to smell the fresh honey, then she drops to her knees so hard Anthony flinches for her. She stuffs the brain-chunked honey into her mouth with her grubby hands.

The bees calm when the honey is gone and she slumps on her mattress, exhausted.

All it had taken was one errant branch, one cursed moment, for a bee to find its way in.

But he had learned that honey from another Hivemind keeps the queen from laying eggs, keeps the number of bees down, the damage to the brain minimal.

Pulling a can of beans from a shelf, Anthony sits on the floor near her and rests a hand on her head, stroking her beautiful blond hair.

He feels her head vibrating with the contented hum of the honey-sated bees. Taking his helmet off and setting it to the floor, Anthony eats dinner. It almost sounds like she's purring as she slowly falls asleep.

She'd begged him to kill her when she'd felt that first tell-tale itch of a burrowing bee. But he couldn't. Not her, not his beautiful wife.

So, Anthony had chained her down here and, in the end, chained himself to her.

She stirs and turns her head. Her blue eyes still have a semblance of who she used to be.

Around the bees sleeping in her mouth, she struggles to form words.

"P…lease…"

"Shhh, my love." Anthony strokes her hair and swallows back tears.

"K…k…kill…me…"

Anthony only shakes his head. Shakes his head so hard, his brain buzzes. As if the bees are in him too. She trembles and honeyed tears run down her cheeks. Both of them, preserved in a sweet, buzzing limbo.

The Space Between

Alyssa Dean's Official Log – 1.16.3105
Entry 34

Our camp straddles the border of Arizona and California, baking in the sun as it sits guarded on all sides by cacti, sand, and scrub. Northwest of us, three kilometers further into the Sonoran Desert, is the Space.

The Space is roughly eight meters by eight meters: a perfect square – unheard of in nature. As far as we can tell, it rises six meters high and we have theorized that it likely extends six meters beneath the surface of the desert as well.

The Space can't be seen by human eyes, but it registers on infrared and thermal imaging, showing to be approximately 98 degrees – normal human body temperature. Apart from that, the Space is invisible, or it is a colour that the human eye can't perceive. In – or through – the Space one can see the landscape behind it. There is no visual distortion to indicate it is there, every cacti, tumbleweed, and scorpion can be seen through it without hindrance.

The first indication the Space exists is made through the human sense of touch, rather than sight, smell, or hearing. Within two meters, one's body hair rises, one's teeth begin to vibrate in one's jaws, and the subject begins to feel a general sense of unease. One meter away and one can detect a deep hum emanating from the Space. It's an unsettling noise, deep enough that it's almost a feeling more than a sound. It gets into your bones and rattles them, it sinks into your organs and numbs them, it stings your eyes, creates headaches, causes toothaches, and has made more than a few individuals faint and vomit – usually in that order.

The most unnerving dimension of the Space is its interior. The Space measures eight by eight by six feet tall on the outside, but step past the flimsy yellow boundary rope staked into the dirt with tent spikes, and you step into an endless country of misty twilight.

It's a bit of a shock to go inside. The Sonoran is stifling hot and dry, but inside it is always cold and damp. The weather never changes, it is always overcast inside, unaffected by desert storms and temperatures. In the same way, no matter what the time of day is on Earth, inside it is always twilight. The humming also grows worse inside. It's unbearable unless one wears earplugs. Visibility is low. The mists shift constantly though no wind exists.

Entering from the North, West, East, or South side brings one to a similar landscape that is completely independent from the others. An orange pylon set in the North side cannot be seen from the South side. A bright light shining inward from the East side is not observable from the West. An individual can call and shout all they want from one side but will not be heard from any of the others.

We don't know how large the Space really is on the inside. Attempts to map the area have failed, twenty meters into the Space and robotic explorers fail and must be dragged back by the power cords. We have, as of yet, not allowed any human volunteers inside to explore. That changes tomorrow morning.

I, Alyssa Dean, employee of the US government and chairwoman of the Humanity Rescue Committee will go into the Space.

I've included my last will and testament with this document in the case of my death.

It's midnight and I should be asleep. In six hours, I will step across the yellow rope into the Space and look for mankind's salvation.

With electronics rendered nearly useless, I will be armed with only rope, two thick notebooks, a dozen pens and pencils, and a dozen sturdy plastic bottles that can clip onto the rope pulley attached to my belt, to be fed back to the outside world as a fail-safe communication method.

Using the notepads and pens, I will describe everything I see and find. If I am lucky, then the Space will be habitable. If we are really lucky, there will be enough space inside to accommodate some of the excess population of this starving planet.

Alyssa Dean's Communications From The Space – 1.17.3105

Entry 1 – the beginning. Carl was the only one who waved as I stepped into the Space. The others – scientists, doctors, soldiers, and civilians all – watched me go without a word, without a farewell. Maybe they all believed I was coming back. Or maybe they saw me as a dead woman walking.

Inside, I immediately felt chilled despite the heavy down jacket and thick long-johns I wore.

There is a smell here. Something not reported in previous tests. It smells like chemicals. It's a subtle scent but cloying. It has the acridity of vinegar with the offensiveness of bleach, underneath it all is a sweetness, like the taste of cherry Chapstick. I've checked my compass. It is also useless in the Space. No matter which way I face, it points forward and doesn't move at all.

Entry 2 – 2 hours in.

My watch is still working and says I've walked five kilometers now. That's if it is correct. No changes in landscape. It's hard to see very far in this shuffling exodus of mists. It's strange how my footsteps echo in the emptiness. It almost sounds like someone is following me, mimicking my steps. A few times, I couldn't help myself, I had to look over my shoulder to make sure there was no one there. Of course, there wasn't anyone. I am alone in here. It is only the echoes of my own steps in the quiet.

Entry 3 – 3 hours in.

Watch is still working. Whatever it is that affects the larger, more complicated electronics may not cause the watch to malfunction. Of course, the larger machines usually broke down at least twenty kilometers in and I doubt I've gone that far yet. I've only gone another half kilometer according to the watch. Am I really walking so slowly? The only reason I know that I am not travelling around in circles is the pulley system tied to my waist. Behind me, the rope lies straight along on the coarse, gray sand. I am able to conclude that I have not strayed right or left.

The smell is stronger. It is getting worse as I walk deeper into the Space. It's almost unbearable so I've been breathing through my scarf. I am taking shallow breaths, sucking the stale air through my teeth. It's foul on my tongue but my nose can't take anymore of it.

Entry 4 – 4 hours in.

I should be out of the Space by now – if it respected any known law of physics that is, but I am still walking.

The ground remains uniformly flat, almost smooth in its sameness. This contrasts with how the Sonoran is – all sloping dunes and shifting sand. I've collected some samples to send back, they are included in the vial in this bottle. An important note is that closer to the border between the Space and the outside, the coarse grit under my feet used to match the colour of the sand in the Sonoran, but now it's gray.

No, that's not exactly right. To be more exact, it's colourless. On the ground, it looks gray, but if you pick up a tiny pebble and hold it up to catch what little light there is here, you can see that it is transparent – like the fur of a polar bear. It only looks dark on the ground, when it is collected up in the thousands.

After making that discovery, I spent a few minutes investigating. I dug with my hands for a bit but couldn't get far. The sand transitions to dust, transitions to hard-pan, and is impossible to get through without proper tools.

This might pose a problem when it comes to moving a large part of Earth's population here. We might have to forgo basements, cellars, anything below ground-level. This means we'll have to build up into the twilit sky instead, as high as it will allow us. Farming – with this perpetual twilight and lack of rain – will be impossible.

Entry 5 – 5 hours in.

I have a splitting headache. I've taken two ibuprofens. My watch has finally stopped working so I am just estimating the passage of time now. I've eaten but it is hard to get hungry. The sound of the Space, it gets into your body and you just feel sick all the time.

Important to think about – will the human body eventually adjust? Or will we need to use this Space for automated plants and factories only? If so, how do we solve the problem of power source? Maybe this Space is unusable. For humanity's sake, I hope there is something we can do.

Entry 6.

A relief: I've adjusted. There is no pain anymore, no feeling at all, no sound, nothing. I'm numb. It's peaceful. Like being asleep while being awake.

Does that make sense?

The peaceful body-feel of sleep. The alertness of awake.

The mist surrounds me on every side. This rope is my only anchor to life. I wonder how far this rabbit hole stretches.

Entry 7.

I woke up on the cold ground. My whole body was

shaking from the cold. The strange, colourless sand and grit had coated my body, crept over me as I slept, trying to bury me. I must have fallen asleep. I feel better.

Entry 8.

No sense of time anymore. My only contact with the outside world is the feeling of people tugging on the rope, bringing my messages back via pulley. No one writes anything back. I wonder what you all think of my discoveries. Please send something. I need to hear from you. It's so quiet here, I feel like I am already dead. Send something back to let me know I am alive.

Entry 9.

A great, dark crevasse lies before me. The ground is split open in a gaping, smooth, moist looking gash. The ground revealed along the sides of this gently sloping chasm is black, completely solid – like tightly-packed clay.

It's here that the stench of cherries and chemicals emanates.

I am sitting on the edge of the pit. I can't see the other side. It must either be huge or the mists hang too heavy above it for me to discern the other side.

I could go around. I could turn back. I could try and get a sample from the dark material in the rift.

I am asking you back in normal space. Advise me please.

Entry 10.

All I am receiving back are empty bottles, sliding through the dirt, pulled by the rope. The plastic bottles shush-shush-shush through the dust like artificial snakes.

I asked for advice, but no response came. I know you are receiving my messages because the bottles come back empty, but you are not sending anything back.

Should I carry on?

Should I come back?

Entry 11.

For the last little while, I've been feeling tugs on the rope. Maybe it's been going on for a long time and I've just only now noticed it. Are you telling me to come back? You will have to send someone along the rope, I can't come back now.

I am frightened.

I went down the gentle slope of the pit, only a meter or two, so that I could get a sample to send back to you. I was planning on turning back after that. You can find that sample in the vial with this message.

You need to send help. There's something down there – in the dark.

The clay was softer than I thought, and now I am stuck mid-calf in it.

Please, please send help as fast as you can.

I can hear it moving.

Entry 12.

I can feel you tugging on the rope. What does that mean? My fingernails are ripped off, bleeding, sore – I tried to claw myself out of this muck, but it didn't work. I can see it moving down there now. I saw red eyes, hundreds of them. They were huge, huge eyes, crimson, bright with intelligence.

I caught the hint of legs – eight or twelve or more, too many – great scrabbling claws – segmented limbs.

There's life down there, but I don't want to see it.

Entry 13.

Its shell stretches on for ages and ages – its shiny carapace is orange, red, yellow spotted with white. A poisonous calico pattern. The shell thrust forward and hangs over an unknown face that sparks with a thousand eyes. Each eye glitters with a malign awareness that makes me shudder. A bottom jaw protrudes from beneath those eyes in a terrible underbite. In the twilight, I can see it bristling with needle-thin teeth as long as my leg.

I think it is emitting the smell. I think it's a lure – like a Venus-fly trap maybe, but this thing is more like a mutated crab, a radiated spider – something not of this world.

I don't know how long it is taking each message to cross the vast distance between us but if you don't get here soon, it will be too late...

i cant wait it will come for me i have to leave

Dr. Deborah Carter's Log – 1700H – 1.17.3105
Patient: Alyssa Lou Dean
Age: 36
Blood type: B-

I am adding this record to the combined files and documents of Dean's journal and records sent back in note-form from the Space.

She returned to us an hour after entering the Space. Her notes lead us to believe that her watch malfunctioned soon after she entered. She believed that she was sending messages on the hour, every hour, but actually sent them at irregular intervals – sometimes five minutes apart, sometimes back-to-back.

Despite the short time that elapsed, Dean spooled out several kilometers of rope – much more than the length of the Space itself. Even if the theory that the Space is larger on the inside than it is on the outside prove to be true, it still wouldn't have been possible to walk that distance in such a short time.

Dean returned almost out of her mind. She was ranting, practically foaming at the mouth, so I was forced to sedate her for her own safety and those around her. The military police brought her into the medical tent and I examined her while she was asleep.

It was strange. To say the least.

Dean was dehydrated. Indeed, she was severely dehydrated. Dean was also suffering from the beginnings of hypothermia. This shouldn't have been possible for the short amount of time she was gone. She was also covered in a thick, pungent mud or clay. This must have been the substance she described in one of her last messages back, though no sample was included as she had claimed in her message. The vial that accompanied the note had been empty.

Her shoes and gloves were gone, her outer clothes had suffered some minor damage, and her feet and hands were extremely dirty. She was also suffering the effects of prolonged frostbite. I had to remove two toes on her left foot, as well as the big toe and two next to it on her right foot. All but two of her fingernails had been ripped off and her finger-tips were stained with blood, which seemed to align with her claim of having tried to claw her way out of mud.

All other evidence remains inconclusive and contradictory.

We are now waiting on the results of the blood tests, as well as her testimony when she wakes up.

I can't explain her condition to injuries. She was gone only an hour our time but is suffering from the physical trauma that a victim of several hours of extreme exposure would. The only explanation is that time must operate differently in the Space – or that Dean's belief in her false perception of reality was strong enough that it caused psychosomatic reactions.

Colonel Roger Penner's Report
1345H – 1/31/3105

Official report of Alyssa Dean's testimony about her hour of recorded Earth-time in the Space. She remained in a coma since coming out of the Space until seven days ago. She is only semi-coherent and requires regular sedation to subdue her screaming fits.

Over a series of interviews, short in duration, I gathered the following from her:

Dean believes she spent close to ten hours in the Space.

Dean believes she sent back samples, though none were found in the bottles.

Dean believes she encountered an unknown lifeform.

Dean believes that she managed to free herself and escape before the lifeform fully emerged from its burrow.

Dean believes she encountered additional lifeforms, over two dozen in quantity, described as miniature versions of the larger lifeform she spotted in the pit – she believes them to be the spawn of the larger creature.

Dean believes she saw these lifeforms tampering with the bottles, taking out our messages that were sent back to her and tugging on the rope.

Other than the above described delusions, I was unable to obtain any useful information from her. Psychologists brought onsite believe that the humming noise generated by the Space affected her mental capacity in the hour she spent inside. This has a grave meaning for the success of our mission. The Space might not be able to host human habitation without negative side effects on the populace.

Further research is required on how to optimally use the Space. Automated food generation plants or robotically-operated factories may be the only option if the power source problem can be rectified. Or the human population without stable housing or jobs may be compensated with a pension in exchange for living in the Space and freeing up the Earth's surface for more productive units of the world.

Upon recommendation in observation of her deteriorated mental capacity by the on-duty psychologists, Alyssa Dean will be relocated to St. Martin's until she is recovered.

End report.

*Alyssa Dean's suicide note – found in her cell at St. Martin's
Home for the Unwell*
Added to the file 3/3/3105

    I hear it chittering in the shadows.

    I hear its claws scrabbling at the bricks at night.

Everyday I can smell bleach and cherries.

    I don't know when, but it will soon be here.

    I won't wait for it.

    No one believes me.

    They will.

    I saw it when they made me leave base.

    The boundary rope.

    The border, colour of buttercups, thick nylon kept in
place with steel rods stabbed into the sand.

    It was gone.

    The Space ate it.

    The Space is growing.

Gemini Syndrome

Mara sighs a bit and leans her head on a fist as she clicks to the next screen on her computer. Her carefully made up and sculpted face is weighed down with boredom. My back hurts from sitting in the stiff, plexicarb chair in front of her desk and I just want this all to be over with. I'm nervous enough as it is and the longer I sit in here, the more I begin to second-guess my decision. Mara sucks her teeth and then continues.

"Last one," she slides a digital scanner across the speck-less surface of her desk towards me. "Upon supplying your thumb scan, you understand and acknowledge that your decision to travel by way of Dispersed Molecular Travel (hereby referred to as DMT) is wholly voluntary and you understand and agree that participation in DMT carries with it the risk to you of grievous personal or bodily injury (including death). Furthermore, you willingly and knowingly accept that risk. You also understand and agree that Vulpes LLC does not and will not guarantee your safety during your participation in DMT."

A pause. I open my mouth, but she holds up a hand. Sucking in a deep breath, she continues.

"With this understanding, you, individually, and on behalf of your heirs, successors, assigns, and personal representatives, hereby release, relieve, indemnify and forever discharge Vulpes LLC, its employees, agents, officers, trustees and representatives," she says. "From any and all liability whatsoever for any personal or bodily injury (including death) that you may sustain, including but not limited to any claims, demands, actions, causes of action, judgments, damages, expenses and costs, including attorneys fees, which arise out of, result from, occur during or are connected in any manner with your participation in the DMT."

Another pause. I wait longer. Mara looks up at me from her computer screen.

"Place your left thumb on the scanner if you agree to these terms," she says with an eye roll.

I am about to say something in response, likely something snarky, but restrain myself. Instead, I place my thumb on the scanner. It flashes blue and beeps. Mara reaches out, snatching it from under my hand, and places it back in a desk drawer. There is more silence as she clicks through something on her computer, then she nods.

"You're good to go, Officer Burnett. Your departure time will be today, at 1500 hours. You will report to the DMT testing lab and be given further instruction there. You cannot

. take belongings with you; I will ship them out to you on the next shuttle to Earth. Be at the lab twenty minutes before your departure time. You understand?" Mara says, leaning back in her padded chair.

"I understand," I reply, my voice wavering, and my heart pounding viciously in my chest.

"Alright. Thanks for your service here on Omnikron III and safe travels," she says, as mechanically as the systems I had serviced these eight long years.

I can tell when I've been dismissed so I stand, stretching out my legs. I feel my lower back pop and wonder if she hears it. As stiff as her dismissal, I walk out of the HR office and into the gleaming white hall. Cadmus and Naab are waiting for me, leaning against the panelled siding, arms crossed, and heads together as they whisper. When I exit, they look up, their faces maps of concern.

We stand, a beat of a pause. Then Naab breaks it by clearing his throat, offering a weak smile.

"Still going through with it then, Pru?" he asks.

Cadmus is looking everywhere but me. It's obvious he's still furious that I had refused to sign a supplemental contract, that I had refused to stay here with him.

"Yes, I'm set for departure in two hours," is all I can say, because I can't tell them how frightened I am.

"Are you going to make the rounds, say goodbye to everyone then?" Naab asks, stuffing his hands into the generous pockets of the standard issue jumpsuit he is wearing.

The thought of dealing with the worry on everyone's faces, their questions, their speculations, makes my stomach drop low and my mouth dry up instantly.

"No," I force a laugh. "They know I'm planning on heading out and I hate goodbyes."

Cadmus clears his throat.

"Let's head to my bunk then. We can celebrate," he says, sounding as dire as a dirge.

"I scored some homemade scourge from Smithy. We can send you off proper," Naab smiles for real this time.

The initial nerves have passed and I take a deep breath to further steady myself. I can match his smile naturally now.

"Sounds good. I think I deserve a proper farewell, considering I'll be one of the first pioneers of DMT in the interstellar realm," I say.

Cadmus takes the lead, walking fast, and leaving us trailing behind. We pass other crew members dressed all in the company issued jumpsuits. I nod at the faces I recognize, but don't slow down, afraid they might start asking questions about my upcoming trip and spark off my nerves. The halls of the station are humming with sound, familiar and almost comforting – the susurrus of air recyclers, the whisper of distant conversations, and the low grumble of the energy core. Once we enter the dormitory corridor, Naab splits off to his own room and I follow Cadmus, alone, in silence. He doesn't look back, but I don't need to be led either, I've been to his room many times after all.

Once we step inside, Cadmus finally turns around.

"So that's it. Were you even going to say goodbye?" he says, his voice trembling.

"You knew I wasn't planning on extending my contract," I say, crossing my arms, feeling cold.

"Then this meant nothing?" he gestures around. "I meant nothing?"

"Your contract is up next month –"

"Stop," he says, his voice rising. "Stop it, Pru. I'm not insane like you. I won't be risking my life with DMT. You've heard the rumours. Everyone has."

"They tested it," I really wish Naab would show up.

"They tested it on Earth. And it was fine, but when they took it out here," he gestures again, vaguely, impotently. "That's when the tests began to fail and, what, you're willing to risk it rather than go into hypersleep for a decade?"

"Rumours. That's all they are: rumours," I say. "There hasn't been a single recorded fatality or injury as a result of DMT."

He shakes his head.

"And you trust Vulpes to be honest about the result? If it means it would slow their development? It would put a halt to their experiments?"

Naab walks in, holding a small green plastic bottle, and completely oblivious to the tension in the room. He shakes the bottle.

"Cheers to Pru, soon to be Earth-side, breathing dirty non-recycled air and eating fast food – what I wouldn't do for a burger!" he says and lifts the bottle up in the air, before taking a swig.

He passes it to me. I follow suit. The scourge burns hot down my throat and settles in my belly like a coal. I offer it to Cadmus. He reaches out, our fingers touch on the bottle, and he lets them linger. Guilt gnaws at me. If I was in love with him, I know I should feel something, that this contact should inspire something ... more.

But it doesn't.

I slide down the wall to sit on the cold plexicarb floor. After a moment, Naab and Cadmus follow suit.

"I'm gonna miss you, Pru," Naab says with a sad smile. "I plan on signing up for another extension, so I won't be seeing you Earth-side anytime soon."

"You're addicted to this sterile life," I say, with a small laugh.

"It's a comfortable life, structured. Plus, I always had the worst allergies on the planet. Here," he takes a long sniff, pauses, then shrugs. "Perfecto!"

From where I sit, I can see through Cadmus' bunk window. Beyond is only a cold, comfortless darkness. The ship, too, is comfortless. It is like a buzzing eyesore, all gradients of white, gray, and black. A sterile prison where I and the others work like ants.

I close my eyes; I try and imagine Earth. The Earth I knew, from eight years ago. The tall gray cities of concrete and glass, baking asphalt and humming vehicles. The trees, the smell of fresh rain, of pollen in spring. It's all gray, faded, distant. My nerves strum and I desire nothing more than to experience it all again, like for the first time. I try and picture my father's face, his corny jokes, his braying laugh. The back of my eyelids prickle and I push my thoughts away.

I shake my head and take another swallow of Naab's acquired scourge when it comes my way, knowing I shouldn't, but wanting to tone down the ringing of my thoughts.

"I don't think you should take DMT back," Cadmus says.

"Please, just let it go, okay?" I say, opening my eyes and

checking my watch. "I've signed the papers, I've my appointment set, I am going to be home in a matter of hours now."

"I can understand his worry, Pru. This is a relatively new mode of transit so, naturally, there's been a plethora of tales going around about it," Naab says with a sympathetic shrug.

"You could die, Pru," Cadmus says, grinding the knuckles of his right fist into his forehead. "I can't believe there's something on Earth willing to make you risk your life."

I shake my head, staring up at the ceiling. Without glancing his way, I hold out the bottle to Naab, who takes it without a word.

"We could die up here at any moment too. Life support failure, impact with a stray meteorite, core malfunction," I'm being flippant to hide the anxiety that's flaring up, doing anything I can to hide my own fear so it doesn't encourage him into thinking my mind can be swayed. "Life comes with risks, Cadmus. I want to go home. I want to be there now and not in a couple decades."

I check my watch again. A shiver runs from the crown of my head to the tips of my toes. It's time. I clear my throat and stand.

"I can't take any of my stuff with me," I say, forcing a smile on my face. "You guys should go through it and see if you want anything. It's all yours."

"One last one?" Naab stands and holds out the bottle, nearly empty.

I shouldn't.

I take the bottle.

"Thanks," and finish it off.

"Let us take you to the lab," Cadmus leaves his room before I can protest.

The walk to the lab is going to be a long one. I sigh. I look up and Naab is watching me carefully. He reaches out, wrapping his arm around my shoulders, and giving me a brief side hug.

"His heart is breaking," he says. "Forgive him his pain. Be kind. This is the last you'll ever see of him after all. Or if he does go home after his contract is up, you'll be decades older and he'll be the same, and still in love with you after you have moved on."

I sigh.

"This is hard on me too," I say, though I know he'll assume it to be for other reasons than what it actually is.

"I'm worried too," he continues. "I know they're just rumours, but don't all rumours have a nugget of truth sometimes?"

"They wouldn't allow people to travel with DMT if people were dying from it, plus I looked into all the people who've done it previously. It's all public record, as required by law. I emailed them, they're fine. You can do the same if you want. The worst thing that happened was one of them suffered some bad nausea and ended up puking on one of the receiving crew members."

I'm talking way too fast and I can't tell who I'm trying to reassure right now.

Cadmus slows down to let us catch up. His fingers find mine, become entangled, and we walk side by side like this, down the hall. My palms seem to grow sweatier the closer we get to the lab.

He must feel it because Cadmus looks at me, his eyes soft and concerned.

"You can still back out," he says.

I suck in a deep breath.

"It's just nerves," I reply.

"But why?" he pulls me to a stop, taking both my hands in his and holding them tight.

"My father is dying, Cadmus."

My eyes begin to tear up and a lump grows in my throat.

"Pru, I – I didn't – you never said anything," he says.

Naab has turned his back to us, giving us what privacy he can, pretending he isn't a witness to this. I clear my throat, trying to swallow back the tears.

"He only just emailed me a week ago. The prognosis has gotten worse. Originally, he had hoped that he would live long enough to see me get home via ship," I shake my head. "You know he inspired me. He was the one who made me fall in love with all this: space, quantum mechanics, every-thing. I just – I need to see him one last time. I want to tell him I love him, in person."

Cadmus pulls me in, wraps his arms around me. The emotions threaten to spill and I want to escape, but I give him this last moment. After all, Naab is right, this is likely the last time we'll see each other. So, I give him this one last moment and concentrate on choking back the tears.

Eventually it is Naab who breaks us up. He clears his throat.

"You're going to be late for your flight, Pru," he says and Cadmus allows me to pull away.

I turn and look at the door to the lab. It is a tall and daunting slab of steel that slides into its pocket in the wall with a hydraulic hiss when I hit the button. A man wearing a lab coat over his jumpsuit is waiting.

"Pru Burnett?" he asks, checking his clipboard.

"That's me," I say.

"Come on in. We're ready for you."

I turn to Naab and Cadmus.

"I'll eat a cheeseburger for each of you," I say, in lieu of a goodbye.

I turn away and flee into the lab before my emotions can catch up. The hiss of the steel door closing behind me is both reassuring and foreboding. Like a coffin lid closing on my former life, here on Omnikron III.

"I'm Dr. Einarsson and I'll be walking you through your departure." The man says, leading me briskly past computer consoles, machinery, lab equipment, to the very back of the lab.

It is here that several other scientists have gathered, standing in front of a large control panel with several display monitors. They look up at me and smile. I want to be reassured but there are also two armed members of the company's security crew standing off to the side, carefully watching me.

Near the back wall are nine-foot-tall rods set in a semi-circle, connected at the floor and ceiling. Mounted on each one is a mechanical apparatus, much like an arm, currently pointed towards the ceiling. From the joints, I can only assume they move. In the middle of those rods is a small platform, brightly lit from several floor mounted lights.

"We'll have you change into these," Dr. Einarsson says, holding out a bundle of gray fabric. "They allow the DMT machine to scan more effectively."

I take the clothes and he gestures to a tall screen off to the side of the room. I retreat behind it and unzip my jumper, stepping out of it and getting into the skin-tight top and shorts. The whole outfit is constricting to the point of discomfort.

I step out from behind the screen, feeling naked being out of the company uniform. Dr. Einarsson is waiting for me and I make my way to him, barefoot.

"Excellent," he says, giving me a once over glance. "Now, if –"

"Is it true?" I blurt out. "What they say about DMT? That some people have died from it since it was implemented for use out here, in space?"

Dr. Einarsson pauses. He glances at the other crew members and turns back to me. He smiles, his teeth white and bright in the artificial light.

"I'm sure you can understand that, since this is a newer technology, a lot of people have some reservations about the whole process. Which is understandable, of course."

I cross my arms and huff out a breath in frustration.

"That's a great company response, Einarsson. But could you give it to me straight? That security detail isn't there just for shits and giggles."

To his credit, he doesn't flinch, but instead smiles.

"We are on a bit of tight schedule. Do you mind if I explain while we prep you for travel?" he asks.

"Sure. But I reserve the right to back out if I don't like what I hear," I say.

"'Course," he says and gestures me towards a compartment, which resembles a large standing shower.

"If you'd step inside? We'll be coating you in a gel that will allow the Dispersed Molecular Travel software to scan you fully," he says.

I step inside and spread my legs and arms as directed. Einarsson continues on.

"DMT was successfully tested on Earth years ago, I'm sure you're aware of that."

I have my eyes clenched shut so I don't know if he sees my nod. Verbal responses are rather impossible as nozzles begin to coat me with a gel that reeks of artificial lemon scent.

"Well when Earth-side testing went well, the company moved our sector to Omnikron III. DMT still works, but there was an unexpected side effect and we are still working to resolve that."

The nozzles cut off and I open my eyes, grimacing at the stickiness. I feel warm, as if the gel is slowly suffocating my skin. Einarsson opens the stall door and I step out, my bare feet sticking to the floor.

"What side effect?" I ask.

"Come over here, please. Right to the base of the platform. We'll wait for the gel to set a bit before having you step up," Einarsson says.

I go to where he indicated, right in front of the gleaming platform. I resist the urge to cross my arms, afraid my skin will glue to itself.

"The side effect, Einarsson?"

"Nothing major. A bit of duplication, is all. Something we've come to call the Gemini syndrome. Likely caused by stellar interference when the DMT transmits a person across the stars," Einarsson retreats back to his control panel and begins tapping away at the keyboard.

"And what do you mean by duplication? What does that even mean?"

Behind me, the machine begins to purr and I feel the floor shiver beneath my feet.

"Well, the DMT scans your cellular structure and deconstructs you down –"

"Can you get to the point, Einarsson? I thought you said we were pressed for time?" I snap, looking over my shoulder at the machine that looms over me.

"The DMT breaks you down and remakes you at the destination point. However, since we've moved it to Omnikron III, the tech has also begun creating a duplicate of the subject at the departure point. Do you mind stepping up onto the platform, please? We are ready for departure," Einarsson smiles at me, but I can't help but notice that the security detail has stood at attention, as if readying themselves.

"You mean, there'll be two of me?" I shiver.

"No, not at all. We have made a few recalibrations so I am confident that we have resolved that issue entirely. Now if you're ready –"

"Not quite yet," I snap, my voice rising. "What happens if your calibrations are still off? Are there going to be two of me?"

"Of course not," Einarsson says. "You'll be Earth-side, enjoying the sunshine and real air."

"And the me that's left here? What about her? What happens to her?"

"The material that's left behind isn't a real person,

Officer Burnett. It's just some bio-waste that'll be disposed of. Nothing to spare a second thought about. Now, I really hate to rush you, but we do need to get moving right away if we're to complete this today."

I turn around and look up at the rods that surround the platform, which are now pulsing a bright yellow.

"You don't have to travel via DMT, you know. There's a shuttle leaving tomorrow. You'd be home in about twenty years, that's not too bad," Einarsson says, in a bored tone.

I think of Dad and square my shoulders back, stepping onto the platform.

"Please face forward."

I turn around and squint in the blinding light of the floor lights. The whole platform is vibrating with whatever hidden machinery lies beneath it.

"It's going to get a little loud in there. I'm starting the DMT and it's going to do an initial scan," Einarsson calls to me.

I am not given time to reply before the machine begins, growling into life, deafening me. The internal gears begin to clank and the mechanical arms attached to the rods that surround me, descend. The rumbling grows louder and the arms shift up and down on their respective rods. It is a claus-trophobic feeling being surrounded by the many limbs of this strange machine. It seems to take ages before the noise lessens and the arms stop at chest level. Einarsson's voice comes through the overwhelming cacophony from some speakers set high above me in the ceiling above the platform.

"Alright, Officer Burnett. We're all set. When the process starts, you're likely to experience some slight discomfort. Previous travellers have described it as really intense pins and needles. Not to worry, it's completely normal and rather brief. Nod if you're ready."

All my nerves are humming and I feel nauseated. For a moment I regret partaking in Naab's farewell scourge.

I close my eyes and nod.

"Understood. Have a nice trip, Officer Burnett!" Einarsson says, cheerfully.

A moment later, the noise level kicks up even louder. I keep my eyes closed and concentrate on taking a deep breath in, a deep breath out, over and over again. The gel that coats my body seems to spark with electricity and my skin tingles, softly at first but then painfully. I grit my teeth. Einarsson was being extremely conservative when he said it would feel like pins and needles. The intensity of the pain increases, throbbing through my skin and into my muscles causing them to spasm. It spreads deeper yet and now my bones ache and my organs cramp.

Finally, thankfully, the feeling fades and so does the sound of the DMT machine. I open my eyes, or, at least, I think I do. I see nothing. It's just black. All around my body is a strange rushing feeling, not of wind or any temperature, just a sensation of intense, powerful movement. This has to be the DMT and I imagine my cells shooting through the cosmos like stars. I wonder at my ability to wonder, that my mind should continue to function as I travel this way.

My entire being shudders as the movement abruptly jerks to a stop. I feel something akin to pain, a bright, detached agony across my deconstructed nerve endings. Have I landed? I wait for the pins and needles sensation that I felt during the initial process. Instead I feel something I can only describe as a rejection of some kind, and then a violent propulsion backwards. My nerves are screaming and I want to join them.

There is a colossal wrench, and a hot wave of pain over my skin, and then I'm blinking in a blinding light. I open my mouth to scream, but my throat fails, and I utter a pathetic squeak instead. I stumble forward, my gel-coated feet slipping on the floor, and then I'm falling. I hit the floor hard, but am thankfully out of the light.

"Looks like she landed successfully on Earth. Just received a confirmation message from Dr. Crable," I hear Einarsson say.

"Shame the recalibrations didn't solve the issue," comes a response from someone else.

My limbs feel like they're made of rubber but I manage to struggle to my hands and knees. My eyes adjust and I look up, squinting past the spots in my vision.

My heart sinks, I'm still on Omnikron III, the DMT failed.

"Dr. Einarsson," I say hoarsely, fighting back a wave of nausea.

He's not looking at me, concentrating on his screen instead. The other crew members are also looking everywhere but me.

"I'm convinced it has something to do with the radiations between us and Earth. If we compensate for it in the right way, it should prevent the duplication," he's saying.

"I thought Dr. Crable thought the Gemini syndrome was more likely based on interference from the neighbouring dark nebulae near the station," says a female crew member standing next to him.

"Einarsson!" I cry.

He finally looks up and frowns. I don't like the way he looks at me. Like I don't belong, like I'm... not human.

"What happened? Why am I here?" I ask.

"Do you mind, Davis?" he says and looks back to his screen.

One of the security officers steps forward, face stiff with distaste, and his left hand unclipping the gun at his waist. My heart drops into my stomach and I'm drenched with a cold sweat.

"Wait, Einarsson! It's me! Pru Burnett! Stop!"

I shove myself backward and push away from the approaching officer. My back hits the DMT platform and I hold my hands up against him.

"Wait, okay? Just wait, please! It's me! I'm not a copy! It's me!"

"Why do these things always say that?" the officer stops in front of me, looking back over his shoulder at Einarsson.

"I'm not a thing, goddamnit! You sent the copy to Earth!"

The scientist shrugs, ignoring me.

"Likely a survival mechanism. Can you just take care of it? We have another person coming in about a half hour for travel," he says, as casually as someone asking another to do some paperwork or to start a new pot of coffee.

"Please, Einarsson, just listen. Listen, okay? Listen to me!"

The officer pulls the gun out of its holster and aims it at me, a frown on his face.

"Please," I look directly at him, willing him to see me for the person I am. "Please don't do this."

His hands are trembling.

"Don't listen to it, okay, Davis?" Einarsson snaps. "Just

get rid of it. And maybe put in a request to be relocated to a different sector if you can't follow simple orders, okay?"

Davis sighs and steadies his gun with both hands.

"Listen, Davis," I say, the tears finally streaking down my face. "I'm not a copy. There's been a mistake, they sent the copy to –"

And the gun goes off.

He didn't even do me the decency of aiming for my head. I fall against the platform, my head bouncing against it with a thunk that echoes through my skull. The pain starts as a hot coal in my chest, then blossoms into a blazing nova of agony. I slide to the left and land onto my side, curling into a ball around the pain center. My hands clutch at my chest, are coated in my own hot blood, the same blood that bubbles up my throat and plasters my lips with the taste of copper.

Davis bends towards me, grabs my ankles, and begins to pull me along the floor. As I'm pulled past where Einarsson is still tapping away at his screens, I reach a crimson painted hand out to him. My head is buzzing and icy waves crash over my body as my muscles tremble.

"You know where the biohazardous waste disposal chute is, right?" he says.

I don't hear Davis' response. My vision clouds and my arm falls to the floor. Limp, I close my eyes. I can hear my heartbeat, first thundering in my ears, then slowing, stuttering, faltering. I think of Dad.

I hear something metallic sliding. Hands under my arms.

I moan and try to reach for them.

I try and beg Davis not to do it, but the blood is still thick in my throat, choking me.

I'm lifted, I'm shoved, and then I'm sliding.

A sharp impact crunches me into a fold I'm not supposed to be in. I hear my bones snap as well as feel them go. The pain is bright and dark at the same time, my senses short-circuited. One last thought flickers: will Dad notice the me that landed Earth-side isn't me? And then there is only darkness.

Planet of the Hungry

Part I: The Star Which Fell

I looked down, into the hole where I had wanted to find a fallen star. Instead, metal glinted in the hazy light of the two moons, partially sunk into the red sands. I slid off my bloat-mule, boots crunching as I landed. K's left-most head lipped the stones for lichen, slobbering gray globs of saliva every-where, while the right-most watched me attentively. Its dead head hung in the middle, staring at everything and nothing, barely more than the size of my forearm and much lumpier. I placed a hand on K's quivering side, in between two plump tumours that hung from the bloat-mule's black-haired flank. The beast stilled under my touch.

Alert, I looked around me, over the shifting dunes, for any sign of danger. The desert stretched out until it was lost in the night.

Below me, in the hole, the metal thing hissed as a door slid out and open from its side, releasing a thick fog. I placed my hand on the butt of my lazgun, going still, waiting. A figure emerged. I readied my gun.

I watched the figure fall to the sand, it floundered, stood.

It was a woman. I could tell by the lines of her face, of her body, highlighted by the moonslight, under the loose white gown she wore. She was bareheaded and wore thin slippers.

I waited. I sucked in the dry air, tasting smoke, scorched metal, the musk of K.

She looked up at me. I stumbled back, my heart beating against my chest.

"For what you hunger?" I said the ritual greeting.

"Nothing, dear stranger. I hunger for nothing. I am here to help," the woman replied.

I trapped air in my lungs and looked her all over. She was plump, well-fed, her hair hung in soft curls down to her waist, her skin was unlined from the sun's touch. She spoke strangely, her voice dancing.

"May I come up? Will you help me? I am unaccustomed to the gravity on this planet," she said and smiled.

I licked my lips, tasted the sour salt of the sands. Behind me, a bird cried out. I felt the sweat on my forehead, I felt it trickle down my back. Even at night, the sands were hot.

"Who you?" I snapped.

"My name is Celine. What's your name?"

She waited at the bottom of the pit, one hand on the

side of the metal box. I focused on her eyes, looking for the flicker of quicksilver that betrayed those with the feed-impulse. Nothing. Her eyes were a deep brown, bottomless. I took my time and looked at each part of her face.

Her skin was smooth with no sign of mesh, her eyes wide and without augments, her lips uncracked from thirst, her hair clean and flowing.

"It's nice to meet you. Though, can I say that without knowing your name?" she said.

"Nan," I readjusted my grip on my gun.

Behind me, K sneezed. Hot goblets of snot splattered across the backs of my thighs.

"Oh! Is that a mammal from this planet? May I see?" Celine took a step towards me.

I matched with a step backward, my finger stiffening on the trigger. She stopped, raised her hands.

"Sorry," she said.

I looked her over again. She was beautiful. I chewed on my bottom lip. It was easy to see she was unarmed. The moonslight highlighted her form beneath the gown. I could see everything, like she was naked. I sighed.

"Come," I kept the gun up.

The woman pulled a bag from the metal box and made her way up, scrabbling in the dust and dirt, then she stood in front of me, still smiling.

"Nice to meet you, Nan."

I let out a hissing breath.

"From?" I asked.

She laughed a bit, pointed to the sky. I looked. There was a bright light between the stars, going eastward.

"That's the CSS Sybil. A carrier ship housing three hundred thousand more people like me," Celine said.

I lowered my lazgun. Stared up at the light as it passed the stars and moons.

"From space?" I gritted my teeth, thinking of the right words. "Why here? Why come?"

Celine stepped towards me. I refused to flinch, to show weakness. I stood my ground. She looked down to my feet, her gaze followed my body up, up to my head. Our eyes met. She reached out with her left hand and touched my graft-arm, stroked its mesh-skin with her fingertips.

"So, what we learned was true. The people of this planet really are part machine."

I took a step back, taking my circuitry out of range.

Somewhere, beyond the dunes, I heard the wavering call of a Starved. I strapped my gun against my side again, went to K's flank. About to mount, I looked to the strange woman. She would die.

I pulled myself up K's dark flank, into the saddle I had made myself. The woman padded over the sand and ran a hand over K's skin, which stretched over its various lumps and cysts. She touched one of K's larger tumours gently, causing the pus inside to shimmer. K's right-most head turned and stared at the woman from the sky with watery gray eyes. The call rose again. I lowered my graft-hand.

She took it and I pulled her up to sit in front of me on the saddle. K's two alert heads snorted at the weight, but it did not buck. I kicked my heels in, urging the bloat-mule on. It kicked up a cloud of dust, taking us away from the Starved and out of the dunes.

I took the woman to the cave I'd set camp in, to escape
the Starved and the rising sun. I knelt at the mouth of
the sandstone cave and closed my nat-eye, allowing my
graft-eye to focus. I narrowed it, centered on the group travelling along the sands. The rising sun caught the quick-silver
in their eyes, erasing any doubt. Starving.

The sun scorched their naked bodies as they scrambled
up a crumbling dune, their spines raised like jagged stones
down their strangely elongated backs, their ribs like savage
cliffs jutting out from their sides. Two dozen of them. They
collected like trash on the wind, this was the biggest group
I'd seen.

"Are those your people?" the woman asked.

I hissed, not turning. I watched the Starved. Their heads
swept side to side. Even from that distance, I could see how
their thin, blistered lips were pulled back from shattered
teeth as their nostrils flared, trying to catch any hint of prey
on the wind. K whimpered behind me. It smelled them. The
sun rose and lit the sands into a bloody blaze. I felt the sweat
on my scalp trickle down my neck.

The Starved continued on. Heat did not bother them.
Pain did not stop them. Their hunger drove them.

When they were out of the range of my bioscope, I
sighed. I turned. The woman was next to K, stroking its
right-most head. K's left-most head watched me and its
middle drooled thick ropes of spit onto the stone ground.
I went to her side and gripped her shoulder, jerking her

around to face me. I took her head in my hands, probed for synthochips on her scalp. I worked my way down. Checking inside of mouth for false teeth, shoulders and chest for wires, hips and ass for comms plugs, bottom of feet for receptors. Nothing.

Hissing, I stepped back.

"Untouched," I said.

"Do you mean I am unaugmented? That is true. I am an Acolyte of the Threshold. We hold ourselves free of the influence of machine."

I went to my bag, keeping my lazgun near. Water, sand-nuts, willow'o'reed stems. I ground them together, mixed with a spot of water, made gray paste. Using the fingers of my nat-hand, I scooped a handful to my mouth. It was bitter but filling.

The woman from the sky watched. K watched with four of six eyes.

I rolled my eyes and offered the bowl to her.

"Thank you," she said and ate a scoop.

I saw the face she made, forced down a laugh.

"It good for you," I said,

"How so?" she asked. "It tastes like powdered potatoes with too much sour cream salt."

I watched her neck as she swallowed, how it moved. I felt hot. I shovelled more paste into my mouth.

"I want to tell you about myself, about why I'm here," Celine said.

I took the bowl for myself, leaning against the cave wall. She was plump. I needed the food. She did not react with hunger, not watching the food, or getting aggressive. Test passed.

I scraped the bowl, eating the paste. I said nothing.

"I was sent down to see what I could see. As an ambassador for the people still on the Sibyl."

She had her bag in her lap and pulled out a small box, a bottle. I heard it before I saw what was in the bottle.

My mouth prickled.

Water.

She poured a few drops into the box, capped the bottle, shook the box.

"We can't live on our ship anymore. It's unfortunate, but we were only set up with a finite amount of supplies. We were meant to locate a planet a century ago. We're running on fumes now. We need to settle. We need to find a planet to settle on," she peeled back the lid of the box.

I could smell it. Something exotic, something absurd, something full of flavour.

She pulled a spoon from her bag and scooped out what was in the box. She ate it. Chewed, swallowed, smiled. She looked at me, her eyes dark holes in the twilight of the cave. The woman of the sky held out the box.

"Do you want some? It's nothing special, just macaroni and cheese."

I snatched the box from her before I knew what my body was doing. Like a malfunction of my grafts. I grabbed a handful of the chunky orange slop. The flavour was an explosion. I couldn't identify it, but my tongue was coated in it. I shut my eyes against the tears – wasted water – and swallowed.

"Tell me about your planet," the woman said. "We've orbited it for three years now. The topography seemed standard, if distorted, which can't be helped considering. But what we were most interested in was the people. We watched you and we saw – we saw things we weren't expecting, I guess is the gentlest way to put it."

I stiffened at the tone she used. That soft, untouched creature, what would she know?

"We survive."

A pause. The wind blew past the cave, a hollow fluting on the stone. K snorted from two sets of nostrils, the third dripping clear goo.

"I understand. Tell me, Nan, do you know why people on this planet eat each other?"

I scraped the box, getting orange slime under my fingernails. I scraped the underneath of my nails with my teeth, sucking out every last taste.

"Cannibalism. That's the noun for it. The act of consuming an individual of the same species."

My mouth was buzzing, my head felt light. I leaned back against the rough stone, closed my eyes. In my nose, despite the lack of grafts, I could still smell the taste of the food in the box. Macaroni and cheese. Unlike anything I'd eaten before.

"It's not unique to this planet, of course. What makes this planet different is the prevalence of the act. Hordes of people falling upon one another, happening all over the planet. This is a hungry planet of a starving people."

"The Starved," I said.

"Yes."

"It's in the eyes. Silver, catching in the light. It shows the feed-impulse."

The woman from the sky sighed.

"Yes. We observed that. A savagery in the movement, mutation in the optical nerve, unprecedented growth of the limbs, and a hunger that is never satisfied. Your people fight a slow battle against extinction, Nan. You're fighting against each other to survive."

I straightened, looked at her. I saw her soft features, water-rich skin. I knew, if I ran my fingertips over her scalp, I wouldn't find the tell-tale bump of sandticks. Her skin would be untouched.

I let my eyes linger over the arch of her neck, the gentle curve of her shoulders, the hint of hips beneath the white dress, the bump of ankles. My whole body clenched, tingled up my neck and into my brain. She watched me stare at her. She knew my gaze. She smiled.

"It's a hard world here," she said. "Will you help me? Nan? I can save this world, but I need your help."

Her voice like water over my skin. I shivered despite the heat.

"Help?" I asked.

She pulled something from her bag, laid it out upon the stone. A map. The woman pointed at a symbol on the map.

"Bring me here."

I looked at the lines, the symbols. It was familiar, yet different, from the maps I'd bought from Choel at the trading town of the dunes. I leaned over it, traced a finger over the lines that must mean dunes, of the scratches that must mean the Nettleglade. An X past all. I rested a fingertip on the X.

"Yes," said the woman. "Bring me there."

"You want to go beyond the Nettleglade. The Starved linger there. It is death."

I stood, went to the mouth of the cave. Dust-devils danced upon the dunes, but nothing else. The sun was up, raising a brown haze over the sands. I sucked in the thick, hot air. I tasted salt, reek of cacti, and the heavy scent of K from behind me.

"It is death," I repeated.

I turned. She was asleep. K had lain and she against it, her head resting on the bloat-mule's flank near a shuddering tumour, filled with pinkish pus.

Part II: Through the Nettleglade

She rode in front of me. I felt her body against mine, a warm weight. K followed my direction, heading north.

"What's that?" she pointed.

"Sandpear."

We passed the tall tree, heavy with bright green, poisonous berries. I was glad that the sky woman did not reach out for one.

"You say know this planet, but know not," I hated the harsh, sand-roughened sound of my voice, it was – different than the sound of hers, hers like the sunrise-singers that flew the skies.

"We had the names of what was, not what is now," was her reply.

We passed out of the sands and onto the moss-plains. The moss-plains were gentler, a thick, green blanket dotted with towering sweet-trees and squat, little bushes. I led K to a small river of dark water. Its two heads drank eagerly while the middle head swayed between their gulping throats. I helped the woman from my saddle so we could sit next to the water. I could smell the suckles and foxtrots, flowers of yellow and blue.

I picked a foxtrot and held it towards her.

"This?"

"In the world that was, it would have been a cornflower," she said and pulled another box from her bag.

I had thought about killing her many times. I could leave her body for the Starved and take her bag for myself. From the bulk of it, I knew there must be many boxes of her food. Delicious things of flavour and color I'd never had before. I thought about killing her many times, but always decided against it. She was strange, but she was company, something new and pretty in this world. Something for me, only for me, something special.

Celine had the bottle of water in her hand, dripped the last of it into the box she held. She refilled the bottle from the creek. She worried not of what was in the water, she trusted in the bottle.

"Want," I held out a hand.

The woman from the sky smiled and took a bite. I could smell it. I bared my teeth at her.

"This one is meatloaf," she said. "A common household meal from one of the countries on this planet."

She ate another bite. I looked at the creek. I wouldn't have to waste battery in my lazgun, I could smash her brains out with a rock. She was soft, so soft. I looked back at her. She was holding out the box. I reached out with my nat-hand. Our fingertips touched. From over the smell of flowers, I smelled her. A strange scent…something other.

I looked at her, the folds of her gown hung off her limbs like spiderweb. Her feet, immersed in the dark waters of the creek, were alien in their softness. She mesmerized me, a strange creature waiting to be mauled and eaten.

I took the box. Inside, a brown loaf covered in paste. I scooped a chunk into my mouth and tasted meat. I closed my eyes. I didn't stop until the box was empty.

"Was it good?" she asked me.

The light through her clothes, the line of shadowed limb behind bright, white dress. I was on her. Nat-hand on nat-wrist, graft-hand on nat-wrist. My flesh on hers. She didn't fight, lay limp. I breathed on her neck, her dark hair followed my inner winds, I smelled her.

"I –" For the first time her voice failed.

I rested my lips against her neck.

"I have never –"

I leaned back, my knees between her thighs. Our eyes met, hers glistening.

I pulled back. K snorted. I looked at her, the woman from the sky, as she lay on the rocky turf of the creek and stared up at the stars. Her arms and legs still spread as I had placed them.

Shame burned hot across my face.

"Acolytes of the Threshold choose to withhold," the woman swallowed, I heard her throat click. "We try to remain pure for the One on the Threshold."

It sunk in. I looked at her again. I shivered, licked my lips, and tasted the salt of her. She looked at me, over the dunes of her own body – collarbone, hips, knees – her eyes on mine.

I offered a hand; she took it and I felt something hard and raised. When I turned her hand over, I saw a scar that ran the edge of her pinky to the bottom of her thumb. She watched me look at it, didn't pull away. She closed her hand around mine and I forced her hand open again, running a thumb over the raised scar.

"This?"

"Acolytes must go through an initiation. A test of pain, of sacrifice. Only the special few are chosen. I, with twelve others, were chosen."

To test her, to test myself, I pressed my lips against her scar. She kept her eyes on mine and I felt my skin scream for her. I was the one who pulled away.

K's hooves marked our trail in the marsh as we made our way to the Nettleglade.

Celine sat in front of me again. The back of her skull rested against my collarbone, her ass against my lap, her thighs against mine, and K swayed us both. My graft-arm sparked, the tingles racing up to my shoulder.

I sucked in a breath, bared my teeth, gripped her harder against me.

"Do you have tribes here, Nan?" Celine asked.

I guided K over the islands of gadmoss, trying to spot the quicksink spots before my mount could step in them.

"Humans naturally gravitate into packs. It's instinct. It's why those afflicted do the same."

"Afflicted." I mouthed her unfamiliar words.

"You called them the Starved. The ones who eat their fellow humans, the ones driven mad by hunger," Celine's voice was steady, she wrapped her hands around mine, which lay on K's reins. "My people want to help you. We want to… make this place better."

I shook my head.

The marshlands were heavy with the stench of mould, pollen, and shit. It lay in front of us as lumpy as K's flanks and was spotted with humped gadmoss, spiky reeds, and clouds of bugs. Beneath the dark waters, softly glowing creatures swam in the swirling muck.

I watched our sides. As K picked our way through the patches of land, I spotted a deer. A male, by the rack on its skull, made its way just as carefully as K, only it had eight legs rather than four – one of which hung limply, disjointed, by its side. Its black eyes fell on us, it grew still and watched.

My fingers itched for my lazgun. This stag could provide food for week. I reached my graft-hand back, unclipped the holster, but Celine stilled me.

"Let it go," she said.

She looked over at it, a soft smile on her face, a glitter in her eyes.

"I've food enough for both of us."

I looked over at the stag. It looked at me. There was a moment. Frozen time. It bounded away, a chance lost as its hooves made splashes in the brackish water.

We went on.

"What do you call your home?" she asked.

"This?" I gestured with my nat-arm, out towards the endless sea of bog.

"No, well," she laughed. "I'd love to know what you call this land, but I mean the planet. What do you call the planet?"

Above us, it was the honey-to-bruise-to-black of sunset, in the plains of the swamp. Celine was a warmth against my body, a comforting weight. Her hair smelled of flowers, of a sunrise dew. My whole body trembled, growled, ached. I was hungry, I needed to … I needed more.

My lips pressed against the side of her neck. I felt her tense, yet she did not react. She did nothing. Nothing but talk.

"A world once known and yet forgotten. A world once thriving, now forsaken. Believe. Believe and yet be redeemed, for is it the nature of humankind to thrive when thought broken. For is it not the covenant to cultivate, to generate, to procreate? A promise to future generations, to future dreams, a pact made yet waiting to be made."

I realized then that the woman from the sky must be mad. Her story of people in the sky seeking a place to settle may be true, but this world was beyond saving. Anyone who lived here could see that. I leaned back in the saddle.

The light faded and lanternflies rose, dancing among the reeds. Glowing swamp gas swirled around K's legs. I'd always hated swamp gas. It moved like it was alive, creeping, caressing.

The ground rose, dried, as K brought us past the bogs and onto firm land again. Here grass grew, short and scrubby. Night had fallen full. Back the way we'd come, I heard a

Starved howl. A chill crept down my back, I looked over my shoulder. Fog had risen across the swamp, I saw nothing.

K – I had cut it from its ma's cooling belly and raised it myself – knew all my moods, felt my fear, and whickered in response. Another shriek rose, a different Starved, to my left. I kicked my heels into K's sides, urging the bloat-mule into a trot.

"You're worried," Celine said.

Ahead of us, the scrubland continued. I could see where the Nettleglade began, far from us, just at the edge of this field. The thin, towering nettletrees stood in a thick line, guarding the boundary between scrubland and glade.

The moons peeked up from the land's edge. Another howl. I clenched the reins tighter. K's right head turned, looking out across the grass.

I kicked K's flanks again and set the beast into a gallop. The Starved rose from the low bushes where they had been hiding. Their eyes glinted silver in the moonslight.

"Faster," I told K, keeping my arms tight around Celine.

The Starved were once like me. Then, when a person let the hunger take hold, they changed. Their limbs lengthened, thinned, until ribs showed like a row of trees across the flank. The shoulders become mountain peaks; the skull broadens across the forehead. Their skin thickens and discolours to a mottled gray hide that resists lazbolts and blade alike. Their teeth sharpen into fangs that push blackened lips out. Nails become talons, yellowed and rough.

Once changed, the human is lost forever. All that's left is a Starved.

I looked around us. There were nine of them, charging

through the scrub towards us. I urged K faster. The tall, skeletal nettletrees loomed, their leafless branches clutching at the night sky, scraping at the stars. The Starved were catching up. Their hunger drove them faster than a twice-burdened bloat-mule could run. I smelled them on the wind. The Starved smelled sweet, a rotten kind of sweetness, cloying and overpowering.

K's right head screamed when the beast caught the scent and it kicked up its hooves, speeding up. We flew over the grass and the Starved fell in behind us. Their howls rose in tandem, a solid wall of sound echoing in the night.

We broke through the treeline. The razor-sharp nettletree branches slashed Celine's bare arms, cut open my cheeks, gouged K's flanks. The sap stung in my wounds, driving pins-and-needles all through my body. Still K ran on, regardless of the pain the beast must have felt.

I looked back. Several of the Starved, the smaller ones – less intelligent – stopped, choosing to try and lick the blood from the branches instead of continuing the hunt. Six left still followed.

They weaved through the trees, sometimes on their two feet, sometimes on all fours, loping like an animal. K's two live heads were lifted, its eyes wide and rolling, its nostrils flaring as white foam speckled its lips, while the middle head slapped against its chest. My bloat-mule was slowing, exhausted under the weight of Celine and me.

"Have you lazgun?" I shouted.

The woman from the sky pulled her bag into her lap, rummaged through it. I braced my feet in the stirrups, standing in them and turning, lazgun in hand. Nettletree branches slapped against the back of my hood, sending jolts of pain through my head. I levelled, fired.

The lazbolt flared, a brilliant streak through the air, and struck a Starved in the left shoulder. It didn't pierce its hide, but the impact spun the creature, sending it sprawling to the dirt. Another shot took out a Starved's left eye, splattering the nearby nettletree with yellowish ichor.

K screamed, two of its three throats warbling. Celine leaned to the left, holding something in her hand. She released it.

"Shut your eyes," she said.

A moment later, the night erupted to day. I had not closed my eyes and I cried out at the pain, tucking my face into the crook of my arm. Behind us, the Starved screamed. I had to trust K would lead us true because when I tried to open my eyes, all I saw were spots. I blinked, blinked, blinked.

The vision in my graft-eye returned sooner than my nat. I checked behind me. The Starved had fallen back, clutching their faces, screeching.

K carried us on, then stumbled. K's live heads reared back, four of its eyes seemed to roll back to look at me, pleadingly. Then we pitched forward. I heard a snap, then I hit dirt, rolling. I got my feet under me as soon as I could, held my lazgun in front of me.

K lay on the ground. From where I stood, I could see one of its front legs tangled in the raised roots of a nettle-tree. White bone stood out in stark contrast with K's dark hair. Celine was crumpled on the ground, face to the dirt, unmoving.

Beyond them, in the trees, I could see the thin, ghastly

figures of the Starved. They fumbled through the trees, arms outstretched, seeking through their blindness. I crouched and went to Celine's side, shook her.

She made a small noise, like an animal calling out for aid. I holstered my lazgun and hooked my hands under her arms, pulled, met resistance. I followed her form down and saw her legs pinned beneath K's bulk. The bloat-mule huffed, tilting back two heads to stare at me.

"Sorry," I told it and felt it in my heart.

K was a beast, but K had followed me throughout the world and had been a friend. I braced a foot against K's flank and pushed, pulling Celine at the same time. The Starved grunted at one another. I could smell them again. They were getting closer.

Celine slid with me until I had her free. I shushed her, lips on her ear. She sat up, her white dress now stained with dirt and nettlesap, with blood and sweat. K whined. I turned and laid my hand on its left head, kissed the right on its nose.

"Thank you, K," I said thickly through my tears.

I couldn't risk any noise drawing their attention. The Starved were still roving back and forth, trying to catch our trail again. I holstered my lazgun, pulled out my knife instead. It only took a moment. I slipped the knife in once, twice, into two of K's three necks. Blood sprayed over the gray dirt, sinking in quickly, filling the air with the scent of metal.

I closed my eyes, kept my hand on K's left head until I heard the beast's breathing slow. Somewhere close by, a Starved wailed. I opened my eyes and rose in a crouch, wiping my knife in the dirt to clean it. I took my bags from

K's saddle, pulling my arms through the straps and settling them as best I could.

Celine waited, kneeling near. She offered out a hand, I took it. Together we slipped through the trees. The trees closed in around us, tighter and tighter. Branches pulled at our clothing, snagged Celine's hair. I shot looks back, watching for any pursuing Starved. I heard when they found K, when they started eating. The wet, pulling sound of flesh being ripped from the bloat-mule's body, the sharp crunch of bone breaking, a greedy slurping as blood was drunk.

I gripped Celine's hand tighter and pulled her along, blinking away the tears.

Part III: The Planet of the Hungry

"I'm sorry about K," Celine said.

We were sheltered in the shadow of two boulders, just beyond the edge of the Nettlegrove. The sun rose behind us, casting a long, long shadow over the dirt. I braced my elbows on my knees, leaning against the stone, letting my head hang heavy. I tried to forget the sounds I heard last night. My eyes prickled.

"Stupid beast," I said.

I felt a hand on my shoulder and I straightened up. The heat weighed on me so I pushed my hood back, let the air dry the sweat on my shaven scalp. Celine reached into her bag, took out a white box. She twisted so that she faced me, on her knees. I watched her take a bottle, pour some of what it held onto a piece of cloth. She began to clean the cuts on my cheek, wiping away the dried blood and sap. It stung, but I kept my eyes on her face. Next came a sticky salve that numbed my skin. She finished by running her palm over the stubble on my head, she smiled.

"Your people. What they think the Starved are?" I asked.

Her smile faded and she turned from me, settling back against the boulder.

"We know them to be diseased. They're people who lost their humanity, traded it for a hunger they can never sate," she took my graft-hand in hers, turning it over in her hands.

She ran a fingertip along mesh-skin, tracking the metal pistons, the wires.

"Your people have no graft?" I let her pull my sleeve up to reveal the joint, where the graft-arm met elbow.

"No. None of us have grafts or implants. We have kept ourselves… natural."

Her fingers found the buttons on the front of my shirt. I watched her eyes. My shirt open, she touched the bumpy scar tissue where my left breast had been, remnants of graft-rot from a failed implant. I watched her eyes and shuddered, then I stood, buttoning my shirt up again, and made my way to edge of the Nettlegrove.

My face felt hot, I tried to push down the anger. She looked at me the same way she'd looked at K. A thing of interest, not an equal. A thing to be prodded, but not seen. My face burned hotter. I thought of her giving me her food, like how I had fed K. Keep your animals happy.

I slipped through the reach of the branches of the nearest tree and pulled my knife from my belt. I braced the tip of the blade against the bark and hammered the end of the hilt with my palm. It broke through, then sap began to drip down the blade. I held the knife in place with one hand, reached into a pocket with the other and pulled out a small glass bottle.

It took time to fill the bottle, but I was grateful for the time away. I cleaned my sticky blade off with dirt, sheathed it, and took the bottle back to the boulders. Celine had her map out. I sat down near her and rummaged through a bag to find my flatbread. I ripped off a bite and poured some of the nettlesap on it.

It had a sweet flavour, with a slight tang. I'd heard tale that it would sooth muscle ache and spark energy. I'd also heard that it was used as a way to forget, to find peace. A natural drug. I popped the bread into my mouth and chewed, closing my eyes. My mouth numbed, it was a pleasant feeling. I had made the bread myself, the way I liked it – with extra salt – the mix of sweet and salty made me smile. The numbness spread, my worries melted away, lost beneath the haze of the nettletree's sap.

When I opened my eyes, Celine was watching me again. I offered her the bottle and bread. She took it and copied what I had done. Instead of eating it right away, she looked at the golden sap, which glittered with white nettlepods. She dipped a finger in, scooped out a pod, and pinched it between her fingers, rolling it around with the pads of her fingers.

"Do you ever wonder what this planet used to look like, Nan? What it was in the time before? Do you ever think about the people? The original inhabitants?"

She ate the bread she held, licked her fingers clean. I stoppered the bottle, packed it away. I tried to think of anything I'd heard, wanting her to know me for more than just a tool, I wanted her to listen to me. I struggled with my thoughts, my words.

"The Old Ones lived in endless white stone cities. They wanted not for food or water or heat or light, but hungered always. The darkest corners of their hearts were the seeds to the Starved. They gave this seed to all their children and the hunger laid waste to the world," I said and felt breathless.

Celine nodded and smiled, I felt a flame spark in my heart again.

"Yes," she said. "The people lived in cities and had access to all kinds of technology. They were comfortable and with that comfort, they wanted more. More knowledge, more power, more wealth. They weren't happy with what they had, they fought each other, they fought the land. The devastation was world-wide. Those wealthy enough fled. They chose to try and find other planets to colonize, or to live in orbit on their ships. My people had a vision of returning, of gaining the resources to save our home world."

I looked out, closing my nat-eye, focusing my graft one. I watched the forest line for any Starved, for any movement at all.

"Save. How?" I relaxed my graft-eye, pulled the map towards me, and started planning the final leg of our journey.

"The place you're taking me," she pointed at the mark on the map. "It's one of several power hub stations on this continent."

I stared at the mark with a frown.

"Power hub," I repeated.

"From there, I can change the course of fate. Change

214

one threshold for another so a step forward can take us to a brighter future."

A faint cry rose, followed by the pained squeal of an animal. The Starved weren't close, but I was unnerved. The sun baked down, the horizon danced in heat waves.

I looked at Celine's bare head and frowned. I pulled a length of cloth from my bag and held it out to her.

She looked at it, back at me, her confusion clear. Such a soft creature. I knelt by her, wrapping the fabric around her neck and head, making sure it draped over her forehead enough to shield her eyes. I threw my bags over my shoulders and helped her stand.

We set out across the scrublands, away from the Nettlegrove. Celine spoke of many things: of ships that travelled the sea, the air, and beyond, the splitting of the one moon to two, the tide-drought and the dust years that followed, the Old Ones who tried to breed plant and machine to save the world from hunger. Their failure and the fall of the planet to the Starved.

The scrublands turned to fields filled with shoulder-high grass. Bugs chased after us for our sweat and, overhead, a four-winged hawk screamed. I watched Celine's back disappear and reappear as the grass swished around her, shushing against her gown. The grass baked in the sun, its smell thick and musty all around us. I missed K. If it had been here, its two heads would be snapping at the grass greedily, slobbering, while its third would have collected burrs like a crown. I smiled a bit, thinking about the bloat-mule.

I froze. Turned my head. Listened.

There had been movement. Furtive, stealthy, something hunting.

I lunged forward, grabbed Celine by the arm, and pulled us both down – below the top of the grass. She looked at me and I held a graft-finger to my lips. I listened. The hawk squawked overhead, swerving up and away from whatever was in the field with us. My heart thundered beneath my ribs. I sucked in a deep breath, held it, closed my eyes, concentrated.

Shushing of grass, both sides and behind. Predators being sly. I felt a chill. My graft-arm itched. Still crouched, I sidled around Celine and bit my lip, thinking. Celine tugged at my arm, held something out to me. It was an orb made of metal and plastic. I looked at her, taking it. She leaned in close, her lips to my ear.

"It's a percussion grenade," she whispered, sending my chills lower in my belly. "Twist, set it down, we'll have two minutes to get out of its three-meter radius."

I didn't understand half of what she said, but I understood what mattered. Listening, tracking the movement, I pulled rags from my bag and the bottle of nettlesap. The knife in my graft-hand, I sliced into the palm of my nat, letting the blood flow onto the rags. Knife back in its sheath, I wiped the blood off my hand, pulled the stopper from the glass jar and poured the sap over my wound to prevent more bleeding and to mask the smell.

The Starved caught my scent, they cried out to each other. Bottle back in my bag, I twisted the bomb, wrapped the bloody rags around it. The movement in the grass zeroed in on us. I grabbed Celine's hand, resisted the urge to run and give away our position, and we crept through the grass, away from the bomb.

The seconds trickled away, like the sweat down my neck. My knees ached with the crouch I held, crawling through the dirt. I listened to the Starved as they rushed to where they smelled blood. I heard them fighting each other, I imagined them pawing at the rags.

I heard a small pop then felt a huge pressure that forced Celine and me down, pressed us against the dirt, bent the grass down all around us. The Starved screamed in pain, their voices fading as they were thrown far. I got on my hands and knees. With the grass flattened, our cover was gone. I didn't stop to look behind me. I took Celine's hand and we ran, ran until we reached where the grass stood tall and we could disappear again.

The sun set, casting the world in hues of gold and blood. Deep, shattered shadows grew from the white remains of a city of the Old Ones. Celine and I crouched inside the grass border. My whole body ached, screaming for rest. The front of Celine's white gown was now stained with dried blood, from where she skinned her knees falling in the dirt.

I gestured out to the shattered landscape.

"Home of the Old Ones," I said. "Stone, metal. Death."

"When people became afflicted, they turned on each other. The government tried to control things and they quarantined cities, but the people refused to be trapped and they rioted. So, the government made the decision and bombed the cities."

I tried to imagine what the city would have looked like based on the distant stone outlines, of where buildings stood half-crumbled. I squinted and pretended to see Celine and I walking between the buildings, doing… what?

Holding hands, maybe. Laughing.

Kissing.

My mouth was dry, I looked over at her, and swallowed.

"Your place, it's beyond," I said.

"Yes. The power hub should be just on the other side of this city," Celine said.

"Dangerous," I closed my nat-eye, scanned the city with my graft.

"You think that there may be afflicted in the city?"

I nodded. Shivered when Celine placed a hand on my thigh.

"I know you'll keep me safe, Nan. You're like no one I've ever met before, fearless and strong," she squeezed, smiled. "You blaze like a flame in the night."

I nodded again and swallowed, feeling the delicious shivers running up and down my body. I wondered how she would react now if I pushed her down, climbed on top. Our eyes met for a moment, then I looked away.

"We'll wait. Nighttime, we'll go," I slid farther back into the grass, sat down.

Celine followed me, wrapping her arms around her legs, knees to chest. I pulled out the nettlesap, bread, and ate some more, relishing the numbness. Celine pulled out one of her strange box meals, added water, shook. She offered it out to me.

A heaviness fell onto my heart. I thought of my feeding K. Of a master feeding their livestock, keeping them obedient. I looked at the food, then up at her face.

"You aren't hungry? It's spaghetti, it's one of my favourites," she said, her hand dropping, looking hurt.

"I'm not animal," I hissed, then I bit my lip.

Celine froze, sunk back, placing the box on the dirt. She pressed her face against her knees. I could smell the food but had no appetite. I wanted her to say something, anything. I waited. The sky darkened; the shadows ate what light was left on the ground. Still she said nothing.

"I want you," I struggled. I had spent so much time drifting from trading town to trading town, alone, that I felt out of touch with speech, with words, with people. "See me. See me for me. Different than you, but –"

I pounded my graft-fist against my chest, my words failed me. My nat-eye prickled with tears. Celine's head rose, I froze when I saw the tears in her eyes. She rolled forward, onto her knees, and grabbed my fist in between her hands.

"I do see you, Nan!" she said.

I gaped at her sudden ferociousness.

"You're so beautiful," she continued. "This, this is so hard – I want you to understand that I see you, but I have to do this. I must. Together, we must do this. Save this world and set it upon the threshold of a brighter future."

She pulled a hand back, wiped the back of it across her nose. I stared at the snot that glistened, taken aback by this sudden change in her manner. Gone was the calm, steady woman of the sky. This new Celine blubbered, tears ran dirty rivers down her dusty cheeks. Her nose leaked, she wiped it again.

I grabbed her shoulders, pulled her against me, and ducked my face into her hair, inhaling the smell of her, of dust, of nettlesap. She was more beautiful now than ever.

219

"I do see you, Nan. But this task needs doing. Please, please help me."

I nodded.

"Yes, Celine. I help. Together, to the power hub."

I kept us close to the stone structures, hugging the walls as we crept over the cracked ground. The moons – or the two halves, if Celine's words were true – played peek-a-boo behind the buildings, the shadows ran deep where the silver light did not touch.

I hated this place, this graveyard of forgotten ghosts. I felt the Old Ones behind every corner, heard their gibberings on the hot night wind that whistled through the rubble. There were too many places for a Starved to hide: alleys, in the shadows of the metal structures Celine called "cars", in the skeletons of the buildings themselves. Nearer the middle of the city, I stopped.

Ahead, around the corner of a larger hulk of building, was a flickering yellow light. I felt a chill crawl over my skin. I gripped Celine's arm. She leaned in.

"I think it's a streetlight. Probably still being powered by the hub."

I looked at her, then forward. Licking my lips, I made my way closer. I peeked around the corner. We had passed many metal trees on our way through the first half of the city, but this one glowed at the top. From where I stood, I saw glass, intact. It was there the light came.

I jerked us back into the shadows as a Starved lumbered out of a space between buildings just beyond the pool of light. I held my breath, waiting to hear its hunting call.

Silence.

I listened to its footsteps, dragging in the glass and stone. I backed up, pulled us down behind the crushed side of a car. Slowly, my muscles screaming at the effort, I lowered myself onto my belly so I could watch from the space beneath the car.

The Starved stumbled on, its footsteps slow in contrast with the thundering of my heart. But on it went, down the street and out of view.

I waited a moment, another, rose back to a crouch. Celine reached out and took my hand. When I looked at her, she pointed down a narrow path between two buildings just beside us.

"We can take this alley and stay out of the light," she whispered.

Down we went. My ears and eyes straining to catch any hint of movement besides our own. The alley was short. Long enough to get us past the first pool of light, but I could see there were more. I regretted not circling around the outskirts of the city as I had intended. Celine had pushed for the shorter route, been urgent on reaching the power hub by dawn.

A scream sent me scuttling back to the alley, crushing Celine behind me against the side of the building. More screams rose, approaching. I unholstered my lazgun, Celine's hands wrapped around my arm, and I shoved her away to leave myself free.

"Ready to run," I hissed, not looking back at her.

Beyond, in the maze of stone and glass and metal, I heard the hungry howls of the Starved. But I also heard the terror of a human inside the rising song. I took a deep breath, another, steadied myself.

Closer and closer, the howling came. I heard hooves on the ground, then saw the riders. There were four and they raced out into a pool of light down the street from where Celine and I hid. They rode tall horses, almost pure, based on how mild their mutations were. A fifth horse trailed behind, limping, riderless.

The riders came towards us. From the street they had emerged from, a half dozen Starved gave chase. The lanky creatures howled, speeding along. The ground trembled underneath my feet and glass tinkled to the ground as it was shook loose from buildings.

I didn't need to focus my graft-eye to see what followed the horde. It lurched out from the shadows, seven times as tall as the rest of the Starved. I hissed under my breath. Behind me, Celine gasped.

I'd had never seen one, had believed the tales to be just boogey-legends to scare the young ones.

The monster peered down the street at the fleeing riders, its mottled gray-black skin glistening in the moonslight. Like a person, it stood on hind legs, had hands, but the resemblance ended there. Its body was gaunt, hollowed out, with ribs as sharp as knives. Like its smaller brethren, its fingers boasted too many knuckles, ended in razor sharp claws. Its jaw was distorted, overcrowded with yellowing fangs – so much so, its own blood leaked from its lips. From deep, dark sockets in its elongated skull, yellow orbs burned with hateful hunger. It tossed its head back, its endless antlers gouging the sides of buildings and shattering glass. It reared back and screamed.

I reeled against the sound, resisted the urge to cover my ears so I could stand at the ready with my lazgun.

I remembered my ma's words, late at night as we travelled with the caravan, on the look out for enemies. They rang in my head like the after echoes of the monster's scream. "When a Starved eat a brother, from sated belly will grow another. Know it for the yellow fire in the eyes, for its antlers which wound the skies. If this monster you see, you must flee, flee, flee."

A Wendigo.

The giant ripped a chunk out of the building next to it, brought back its arm and threw the stone after the ones riding towards us. Its aim was true. The foremost rider and horse splattered against the street right in front of the alley in which I crouched. Hot blood drenched me. The other three were forced to pull back to avoid crashing into the huge piece of debris. One of the riders screamed. The Starved fell upon them, clawing up the sides of their horses.

One managed to leap away, tumbling on the ground. They looked up, our eyes met. The scarf around their face had been ripped away, revealing a black beard, fearful eyes. The man reached for me.

"Help us!" he screamed.

The Starved brought down his horse, swarmed over it to him and sliced through the back of his jacket with their claws.

"Help us, damn you! Daughter – pregnant!"

The ground shook as the Wendigo walked down the street, taller than the remnants of the buildings. It moved with the grace of a human, with the intent of a predator. The Starved scattered before it, forming a ring, waiting for their turn.

The man still struggled. I could see his exposed spine catching the moonslight. The other two were still.

"Help," he whimpered.

The Wendigo reached down, scooping up one of the other riders. The person moaned, then began to scream as the monster squeezed. Blood poured from the Wendigo's fist, dousing the street below. The Starved squealed, shrieked, cried out in hunger all around and yet none moved.

"Sarah, no!" the man had rolled over on his back, he pulled his lazgun from its holster and fired.

The bolt went wide, to the right of the Wendigo's head. It paused, tilted its massive head. The rider, Sarah, continued to scream and scream.

I took a step back, deeper into the alley, pushing Celine with me, praying that she would be silent. I tasted the salt and metal of the blood on my lips. All my nerves were on fire, my circuits sparking with tension as I took another step, another.

The Wendigo dropped the woman. She screamed the short way down, went silent with impact. I hoped, for her sake, she'd died.

We were halfway down the alley, but close enough for me to see the Wendigo grab the man. He continued to shoot, yelling as the creature brought him up to its mouth.

"Damn you! Damn you!"

I turned around, now or never, gripped Celine's arm and

raced away. I heard the crunch. The wet slurps. The hooting and cheering of the Starved as the feast began.

The two moons had near disappeared, the night sky was lightening, when Celine and I finally emerged from the shattered remains of the Old Ones's city, home now only to the Starved and their king: the Wendigo.

From where we stood, we could see the endless fields that spread. My heart sank.

"No power hub," I said, my voice cracked.

I let myself fall to my knees, braced my hands against them, my whole body shaking.

"No, Nan. It's there!" Celine hooked a hand under my arm, tugged.

I stood, followed her gaze. A white stone stood amongst the grass.

No, not a stone. It caught the light in a glint only metal could.

"The door to the power hub," she said with a laugh, and we were off.

Because of our excitement, because of my exhaustion, I didn't notice the signs.

I didn't feel the ground tremble. I didn't notice the shadow that fell over us, stretching on and on across the land.

I noticed the smell first.

Carrion sweetness.

At once, time slowed. Waves of cold and heat rolled over me, nausea. I turned and looked up into the face of death.

The Wendigo was already reaching for me. I shoved Celine, sent her sprawling. The iron grip of inhumane fingers wrapped around my body.

"Run!" I screamed and reached for my lazgun.

But it was still in its holster, under the slowly tightening claws of the monster. It brought me higher, higher. Shreds of clothing and flesh hung from its overpopulated mouth. Its eyes blazed in with a foul yellow light. My ribs creaked, I braced my hands against it and pushed.

Its huge jaw opened, revealing a blackened, scarred tongue.

"Fuck you," I told it.

I was glad Celine wouldn't see me die. I pulled back my graft-arm, fist raised, ready to at least land a punch before I went.

A glint of metal in the air, catching the first rays of the sun. I recognized it a split second before the percussion grenade detonated just behind the Wendigo's right antler. I saw the bomb erupt, the air rippling around it like water. The monster's right antler exploded into shards, the left snapped.

Its head protected me from the blast as the Wendigo reeled away from the impact, shrieking. Its grip loosened and I fell, sucking in a grateful breath. Black blood sprayed from its mouth in great gouts, soaking the grass all around it. I hit the ground, back-first, losing that precious breath all over again.

Celine was at my side in an instant. She grabbed my nat-arm and began to pull me, sliding me along the bloody grass. The ground shuddered as the Wendigo fell to one knee. It whipped its head from side to side, clutching it, howling.

Celine dropped my arm, fumbled for something in the pocket of her gown.

"It's my last one," she screamed and pulled out another percussion grenade.

Her hands were slick with Wendigo blood and she struggled, at last twisted and threw it. I struggled to my feet. Together we ran for the power hub.

I risked a glance over my shoulder, in time to see the third and last percussion grenade blow right next to the Wendigo's knee. It screamed so loud I thought the world would split. The monster fell, we fell with it.

I smashed face first onto the grass and gagged on the taste of the Wendigo's blood. I tried to stand, my knees gave out. Exhausted. On my hands and knees, I looked over my shoulder. The Wendigo was already trying to stand. I looked in front, the power hub was still some ways away.

I forced myself to stand. I had to protect Celine.

I gripped her slender arm with my nat-arm and together, we limped over the grass. I glanced back again, watched the Wendigo get to its feet and sway, clutching its head. The left side of its jaw sagged, broken and shattered. Celine broke away from me, racing the last dozen feet to the small, low structure. I struggled to continue, my ribs screaming, my legs shaking. She was at the door, fiddling with a metal pad next to it.

The ground began to shake again. The Wendigo was coming.

Celine finished what she was doing and tugged at the door. It opened to darkness. She held it with one hand, reached for me with the other.

I could smell the monster again. Despite the pain, I began to jog, gripping the side that hurt the most with a hand. A roar chased me. I wouldn't risk it. With everything I had, with my entire being, I threw myself forward, tackling Celine around the waist. My weight pushed us through the door and down a set of stairs into the darkness. I felt a horrific crack in my already bruised ribs and screamed. I fell forever down the stairs. Forever lost in the pain and darkness.

When we stopped falling, I was laying on top of Celine. Above us, the open door showed the morning sky. The light was erased as the Wendigo smashed against the door, shaking the entire world. It thrust an arm through, the only thing that could fit. Plunged into complete darkness, its claws scratched at the stairs. A muffled howl through the earth. Dust fell on my face, stung my open nat-eye.

Celine squirmed out from underneath me.

"There should be a switch somewhere around here, or further on," she said, and I heard the fear in her voice.

Blind, I searched for my bag, found it, retrieved the bottle of nettlesap. I pulled my shirt up and poured it over my skin, letting it run down my sides. I kept my hands away to prevent them from numbing.

The sap began to work, the pain faded to just a whisper, except when I inhaled too deeply. I cried out when the light struck, bringing a forearm up too late.

"Sorry, Nan, I should have warned you."

I squinted, let my eyes adjust. The Wendigo's arm retreated and the whole world shuddered as it slammed into the door again.

"We need to hurry. The people of old built these power hubs to last, but they never anticipated one of... those," Celine helped me to my feet.

We were on a landing, in between two sections of stairs. I saw how close we had come to falling down the second set and swallowed back bile.

"I'll help you," Celine said and down the stairs we went.

The stairs descended deep, so deep that the sounds of the Wendigo's assault faded away.

"I never expected to see one," Celine said in a low, shaking voice.

"Wendigo, eater of all," I gasped out against the pain.

"Well, no more. Not after today."

The numbness settled in deeper and I was able to straighten up, walk with a steadier step. Celine let go of my arm when she saw but took hold of my hand instead. The stairs ended and we went down a hall, its air thick with dust. Somewhere, deeper in the earth, something hummed. I could feel it in the floor. I paused by an open door that opened to a room full of tables and cases that glowed with light.

"Did your people never wonder how your grafts could continue to function? How your machines had power?" Celine asked.

I looked down at my graft-hand, where its internal circuits glowed with a blue light beneath the mesh-skin.

"The scientists designed those enhancements so that they would charge wirelessly. That's why these power hubs exist. There are dozens across this continent, all pumping energy into the air and feeding the machines you use to survive."

I clenched my graft-hand.

"Remember what I said before? About the scientists trying to breed plants with machines, to protect the world from starvation?"

I nodded.

"The nanotechnology was supposed to protect plants from pests and disease, while making them sturdier, more likely to survive droughts. What they didn't predict – or didn't care to prevent – was the technology making its way into the animals that ate the plants."

We passed more doors and, on one occasion, I saw a yellowed skeleton dressed in decaying clothes, lying on a cot.

"The nanotech wasn't meant for flesh, but it thrived, infecting organs and skin and bones and brain."

Celine led us to the very end of the hall and a set of double doors. There was another metal pad on the wall, I could now see the buttons on its surface. Celine tapped at it and something in the door clicked.

"As it thrived, the tech also mutated and with it, the animals changed."

She opened the doors, revealing a large room dominated by a glowing tube in the middle.

"And people?" I asked, following her in.

"Yes, but in a different way. The tech was just as corrupted by its host as its host was with it. But the corruption manifested differently depending on the chemical makeup and sympathetic impulses of the host. For animals, the mutations were mostly physical. For humans…"

"The Starved."

"Yes, Nan. The Starved."

We stood in front of the pulsing tube, next to a waist-high metal counter covered in buttons, dials, screens.

"You will save us," I stated.

"I will save this planet," Celine said.

She turned to me, wrapped her arms around me, and I melted against her. Her hand fell to my waist, then I heard my knife being pulled from its sheath.

"Celine?"

She stepped back and dragged the blade across her palm. The same palm with the scar. She reopened it and her blood pattered to the floor like crimson rain. Close to skin surface, I saw something in her flesh. She offered my knife back to me and I took it, baffled. With a delicate pinch, she removed something small and ignoring her wound, Celine placed it on the metal counter. It was a small blood-slick plastic pouch. She opened it, pulled out the tiny black stick from inside.

"When a human loses their humanity, when they become so overcome by hunger, or lust, or pain, or hate, they become beasts. And what happens to nanotech in beasts?"

"Mutate," I said.

"Yes. Their humanity is gone forever, they become beasts and that – that monster is the result of two different nanomachines combining," Celine inserted the stick into a tiny hole on the top of the counter. The screens lit up, symbols flashed across them.

"This nanotech cannot be removed, Nan. Not from the plants, not from the animals, and not from the people who live on this planet. My people, we call it the Planet of the Hungry, but it used to be Earth. It used to be home."

I watched her, struck at the profound sadness in her voice.

"The only way to stop the nanotech is to take their power away, to shut them down."

She tapped away at the screens. Pressed a button.

The tube's light faded, its throbbing slowed. The

humming grew quieter. Something niggled at the back of my mind. All this talk of machines so small they lived in people, in animals, rolled around. I stared down at my graft-hand, then at my nat-hand. The room's lights flickered, grew dimmer.

Celine stepped towards me, took my hands in hers. I looked at her face and saw the tears in her eyes.

"I am one of thirteen sent to the planet, thirteen Acolytes of the Threshold. Only one of us needed to reach a power hub, only one of us needed to make it to succeed. The program I uploaded will send a signal to every other power hub in range, which will send the signal out again, and shut down everything."

I looked at the tube, up at the fading lights, and back down to Celine's stricken face.

"We will die," I said, tired. So tired.

She sobbed, nodded, and clutched me to her with a ferocity that scared me.

"I'm so sorry, Nan. If there was any other way…"

I gave into my exhaustion, falling to my knees. Celine slid down with me, refusing to let go.

"You take this planet from us, kill us, for your dream," I sighed.

"For them, not us, not you or me, or the twelve other Acolytes on Earth," Celine said. "Just by landing, by breathing the air full of pollen, by eating the food, by drinking the water, we became corrupted. The nanotech is in everything. It's a parasite. Once inside, the host cannot live without it. Without the energy that powers it."

Celine leaned back away from me, her face dirty and wet

with tears. She held my face with her hands, both of them soft and natural. The lights dimmed further. I started away from her when I met her eyes. They flashed with the tell-tale silver of the Starved.

She didn't flinch at my reaction. Only smiled a soft little smile.

"You have it too, Nan. Your eyes flash when you look at me."

I shook my head, slid further away from her on the tiled floor.

"I told you before. The nanotech reacts to more than just hunger. It reacts to hate and lust and —"

"Love," I rasped, watching her flashing eyes.

She nodded, smiled again, and crawled over to me.

"The core will die in ten minutes, maybe a little more," she said, I let her take my hands again.

She placed them on her breasts.

"Sate your hunger, Nan. I want it too. I hunger for you, for everything you are. Consume me, I want you to devour me, I want to be one with you," she gasped.

Her eyes were pure silver, glowing in the darkness as the lights went out. Only the core shed any light now, as weak as it was. The humming had stopped. I wondered what it would feel like when the nanotech inside my body died. Would it be painful, would it be like going to sleep?

My whole body burned, my desire ran wild. I didn't need light, I saw everything. Every line and angle of her body. I kissed her, hungrily, laid her back against the cold floor as the core flickered near us. And I sated my hunger once and for all.

Polychromatic Screams

Captain Abernathy ran down a passageway calicoed with strobing emergency lights, towards the bridge of the CSS Ironside. Somewhere, deeper within the ship, rose a shriek that reverberated within the hull, echoed by others, vibrating, churning, reaching a horrific level that set the captain's bones shivering within their meat casing.

Fear surged through Captain Abernathy's veins, and he ran faster. Ahead of him, a light appeared, creeping along the floor, right by the door to the darkened bridge. Eerie chromatic colours, a light that shivered, breathed. Abernathy cried out, struggled to stop, fell.

The stuttering light grew stronger, its colours so vivid and false. It filled the bridge doorway. Inside, a figure screaming. The captain gripped the welding gun in his hand, pressed the muzzle against his forehead – right between his eyes – and pulled the trigger, releasing a white-hot bolt of flame into his frontal cortex, saving him from what was coming.

Captain Tiggy's screen lit up with an incoming message marked "high priority" from the Vulpes Company. Still resting her head on a hand, she opened the message. She skimmed it at first, then a small smile perked the corners of her lips, and she re-read it. Straightening in her seat on the bridge of patrol ship, the CSS Claymore, Tiggy checked the ship's current stellar coordinates, then opened ship-wide comms.

"Listen up, everyone. A general alert just came in from the Company. First come, first serve, top-tier bounty to retrieve cargo from the CSS Ironside," she said and paused, imagining everyone's ears perking up. "It looks like we are close to the last known location of the Ironside's distress signal. I'm putting up a poll on the ship's intranet. You have ten minutes to post your response."

The console chimed as Tiggy activated the poll and waited. It only took three minutes for her four-member crew to respond with a resounding agreement. It didn't surprise her; the bounty – even split five ways – would equate to nearly a quarter of their yearly salaries.

Kicking her feet up on the polycarb surface of her workstation, Tiggy typed in the coordinates for the distress signal and approved the course change. Then she sent a quick reply to the Company, letting them know the Claymore was on the way.

Behind her, the bridge door opened with a pneumatic hiss.

"So, we're going on an egg hunt, Captain?"

Tiggy turned and gave her Engineering Officer a smile. Officer Cornell was a little over seven feet tall, a result of a bad batch of maternity-booster supplements overstimulating his pituitary gland while he'd been in the womb. He'd killed his mother during birth due to his unnatural size and the Company had provided his father with a large settlement, allowing Cornell to attend the prestigious Academy.

"Sounds like it," Tiggy replied, pulling the message back up and gesturing to it.

"Ooh boy, with the bounty, I'll have enough for the Pleasure Cruise 'round Sirius I've been saving up for," the giant said, giving a contented thousand-yard-stare.

Tiggy reached out with a boot and gave Cornell's left thigh a kick.

"Get out of here, perv," she said.

The CSS Ironside was a week out of their way, but Captain Tiggy was confident they would be the first to reach it. While the sleek Claymore cut through the vast void of space, her crew cleared out the aft cargo space in preparation for the Company's bounty.

Finally, her workstation pinged, an icon flashing to indicate the Claymore was within visual distance of the target, and Captain Tiggy pulled back the thrusters. Next, she activated the holoscreen at the very front of the bridge. The screen hummed, displaying the area in front and to the peripherals of the Claymore's bow.

Around her, the other crewmembers – Engineering Officers Cornell and Greer, Logistics Officer Stag, and Medical Officer Yamamoto – waited to see their quarry. Each had their own idea of how they would spend their share of the bounty.

Outside, the Claymore faced vast darkness, spotted with distant stars that shimmered. Off the port side, some thousand of light years away, was a small, dull purple planet – like a bruise on the cosmos – it was ringed by white, glittery dust, as if the planet were wearing a veil. But there was no cargo ship in sight.

Tiggy frowned, sucking her teeth.

"Captain?" Yamamoto said. "Did the Company provide any information on the type of distress signal? If it was an attack, scavengers may have destroyed the Ironside to hide evidence."

"Greer, run a scan. If there's even a little scrap, we should be able to pick it up. But there's also a chance the Ironside drifted," Tiggy said.

"Yes'm," Greer said.

Under her boots, Tiggy felt the Claymore pulse out its pings, searching for clues. The entire crew held its collective breath, waiting, until something pinged back.

"Confirmation," Greer said. "Ship found, off starboard side, in the asteroid field."

Tiggy deactivated autopilot and began manually navigating the Claymore towards the stretch of shattered rock and mineral. The holoscreen's projectors hummed louder as they struggled to keep up with the movement, its image flickering.

"There," Yamamoto cried. "Something's catching the

light from the nearby dwarf."

Narrowing her eyes, Tiggy scanned the display until she saw the glint of weak light on the metal flank of a spaceship. The Captain grinned, and her heart quickened.

"I'm taking us in for a closer look. Greer, maintain those scans and let me know if any of those rocks get too close to our side," she said.

"Yes'm."

Tiggy circled the edge of the field, which spun and shifted as if the rocks were ancient buoys on a dark sea. Upon approach, the Ironside came more fully in view on the holoscreen.

"It looks intact," Stag said, biting his thumbnail, nervous as always. "At least from here."

The Ironside rested against a larger hunk of rock. Stag was right, the whole of the ship seemed intact, though Tiggy decided they would still go in with suits for the time being.

"Open external comms," she said.

"You can't think the crew is still alive after letting their ship hit that rock, do you?" Stag asked, his teeth clicking against his thumbnail in a way that made Tiggy's skin crawl.

The comms channel hissed as Greer opened it.

"I set it to go out on all frequencies," she said.

"CSS Ironside, this is Captain Tiggy of the CSS Claymore, sent on Company orders. Please respond," Tiggy left the channel open and waited.

The channel crackled and clicked – typical interference noise – then the bridge was filled with a buzz that rose and rose, causing the very hull to vibrate. The Captain pressed her palms over her ears, flinching back against the noise, when it abruptly cut off. She looked over at Greer gratefully, who shrugged.

"That was… unusual," Yamamoto said, quietly.

"Their comms could be damaged," Greer added.

"Any indication their core might be at risk, Greer?" Tiggy continued to bring the Claymore closer, aiming for the Ironside's port-side airlock, which would be safest to enter from.

Greer sent out another scan and peered at the results that returned.

"None, it's intact. No danger of radiation."

Tiggy re-activated autopilot, setting the Claymore to dock. "Greer, I'll have you stay here to monitor the scanners. Stag, Cornell, Yamamoto, you're with me. Yamamoto, bring your portable kit. At this point, I doubt there are survivors, but it can't hurt to be prepared."

"Want me to bring a lasgun?" Cornell asked, and Tiggy nodded.

"Keep it on its lowest setting though," she replied. "Stag, get set up in the airlock, you'll be the one receiving the product. I'll get the trolley for transporting the cargo, we'll meet at the airlock in ten, got it?"

Her subordinates split apart to complete their tasks. As Tiggy retrieved the large trolley from storage, she began to imagine the little vacation she wanted to take with her share of the bounty. She had quite a few weeks of vacation saved up and had always been curious about spa station, Euphoria, which orbited the largest moon of Hephaestus – a planet famous for its sulfuric water.

Lost in her daydream, Tiggy wondered if Yamamoto would go with her if she asked. The Captain felt her cheeks burn as she pictured Yamamoto in a little black bikini or, better yet, nothing – after all, she had heard that some of the hot springs at Euphoria were clothing-optional.

The Medical Officer was waiting at the airlock with the others when Tiggy arrived, pushing the unwieldy trolley. Its original purpose was for loading supplies when the Claymore took a break from patrols to refuel, but Tiggy figured it would work just fine for a bounty retrieval as well.

As she entered the airlock, Yamamoto held out a suit for Tiggy to climb into – the others having already dressed as they waited. Per Company protocol, each crew member double-checked one another's suits to ensure a proper seal. As they did so, the Claymore lurched a bit, sending Stag stumbling against a wall. The sound of the ship's seal engaging against the Ironside's airlock was loud. Tiggy activated her comms, "Greer, we're ready to go."

"Yes'm," came the Engineering Officer's usual brisk reply.

"To make this as quick as possible," Tiggy said, addressing the crew members in front of her. "We'll do a sweep, check for survivors. Yamamoto will be with me. Cornell, you'll be with Stag. Any survivors will be brought back to the Claymore for treatment. After that, we'll retrieve the cargo with Stag here waiting to put it into cargo."

Tiggy waited until her three officers nodded their understanding, then she turned and initiated the airlock pressurization. Around them, the air hissed as it equalized.

The four pressure lights around the airlock door switched from yellow to green and the door slid to the right, revealing a near identical airlock – Ironside's airlock.

"Alright everyone, remember the plan and let's get this

done," Tiggy said and opened the pneumatic door to Ironside proper.

The interior was pitch-black, not even the emergency strip lighting was active, so the only source of illumination were the helmet lights of the Claymore crew. The artificial gravity was also inactive, and Tiggy bobbed upwards, towards the ceiling.

"Want me to head for the core to try and see if I can get the gravity and lights back on?" Cornell asked, bracing himself against the wall.

"It might be easier to ship all the cargo with gravity off, we can just push it all down the hall and then load it onto the trolley back on the Claymore," Yamamoto said, and Tiggy nodded.

"Try and get the lights back on, but leave the gravity off," she said. "Also, since you'll be there, access the black box and get the records. I'm sure the Company will want them."

Cornell nodded and kicked off down the hall, quickly consumed by the complete darkness, so that it looked like an errant star was drifting down the way.

"W – wait for me!" Stag said, pushing off after the Engineering Officer.

Unlike the other Claymore crewmembers, Stag had been born planet-side, which became painfully obvious when the Logistics Officer was forced to deal with a zero-gravity situation. The man scrambled along the wall, pulling himself along like a bug.

"Shall we?" the Medical Officer asked and launched herself in the opposite direction.

Grinning, Tiggy jumped after Yamamoto, slapping the

shorter woman's ass as she passed. The two women leap-frogged each other, flying through the empty, dark passage-ways of the cargo ship, dodging the debris of those who had called this place home – pens, boots, tablets, even a sketchpad.

They encountered the dining hall first, its dark, cavernous space sobered them, quieting their laughter. The air was cluttered with utensils, plates, bowls, mugs, a mini-ature domestic asteroid field to match the one outside the hull. Tiggy was relieved to see there were no corpses.

Still, she and Yamamoto checked the pantry and the cupboards. Tiggy didn't want to imagine what would send an officer cowering into a cupboard, so she was glad those were empty of any human remains. As the two women were leaving the hall, the lights flickered, flashing to life with a blinding brilliance. Now Tiggy could see all the way down the corridor, to where it curved away to the left, towards the aft section of the Ironside.

"Thank you, Cornell," Tiggy paged over team comms.

"See any ghosts?" he paged back with a laugh.

"None yet. Get that black box data, then complete your side of the sweep. We'll meet you in the cargo hold." Tiggy nodded to Yamamoto, and they kicked off again.

The Captain kept her eye out for any sign of the Iron-side's crew. According to the Company, for this run, the Ironside should have had ten.

"Cap, I just ran a scan, and there's no recent record of any kind of hull breach or fire incident," Cornell paged.

"Heard. ETA on completion for black box transferral to the Claymore?" she asked, twisting her body to avoid collision with a bundle of Company-issued uniforms that matched her own.

"No more than five minutes. Want me to parse through to see if I can find out what happened?"

"Negative, priority is the cargo. Greer can review as we load up."

"Heard." And the Engineering Officer signed off.

The Ironside was twice the size of the Claymore, but Tiggy and her Medical Officer were making good progress, slipping in and out of rooms, finding nothing to indicate what had happened to the crew. The interior hull showed no signs of damage and, when Tiggy checked an additional airlock they came across, it showed no signs of forced boarding. After a while, Tiggy almost wanted to find a body, something to help her figure out what had happened. The lack of corpses, of damage, or anything out of the ordinary, unsettled her.

"The cargo hold should be just through this passage," Yamamoto said, the Ironside's schematic displayed on her tablet.

"What do you think of all this?" Tiggy asked as they drifted around the corner, towards the very rear of the ship.

"Of this? You mean the lack of bodies or signs of life?" the Medical Officer responded and Tiggy nodded.

"It's strange. There had to have been at least one person alive a little over a week ago, due to the distress signal being sent. It could have been a foodborne contagion, like what happened a few years back," Yamamoto said. "I have also been noticing these strange shadows, now that the lights are on."

The Captain reached out and grabbed a strut, stopping

her flight through the air. "What do you mean, shadows?"

Yamamoto had been born on a ship and had lived her entire life on ships, rather than any of the more comfortable space stations or colonized planets, and the fact of that showed in how she was able to twist her body about, slowing herself by manipulation of her momentum rather than grabbing a strut.

"We just passed one, back here." Yamamoto retreated down the hall a bit, then stopped and pointed at the wall.

Less agile, Tiggy pulled herself along the wall to get a better view. There, up the white polycarb surface, was a faint discolouration. Pale gray, almost mauve, it was obvious now that it had been pointed out.

"It almost looks like the shadow of a person," Yamamoto said. "I saw the first one in the hall outside the dining area. It reminded me of those really old pictures of the shadows in that Earth city… Hiroshima, I think?"

Tiggy squinted. The discolouration did look like a person, though that might have been the power of suggestion. The top of the stain was rounded like a head and was at the height of an average human, then the shadow expanded out to shoulders. Its right arm was raised as if to cover its face, the left was flung out. This discolouration continued onto the floor, as if looking for the feet it should be connected to. Tiggy shivered.

"It's probably just a coincidence," she said, but she realized she was whispering.

"The one by the dining hall was similar," Yamamoto added.

"Let's get to the cargo hold, no point in worrying over some weird stains," Tiggy said and pushed off again.

The two women swung around a corner, and Tiggy grabbed two struts, full-stop, forcing Yamamoto to bang into her.

"Shit," Tiggy breathed, not bothering to activate comms.

Before her were the double blast doors leading to the Ironside's cargo hold. Composed of lightweight, syntho-metal, the doors were meant to withstand any breach. The cargo doors on the Ironside were mangled. There was evidence of an attempt to bolt it closed: metal slugs the size of Tiggy's fist floated around the doors, some were half buried at sharp angles along the edges of the doors, as if to trap them in a closed position. There was also a haphazard line of welded metal around the outer edges.

But the central seam, despite the multiple bolts, had been forced apart in the middle, creating a small aperture, beyond which was only darkness. A bolt gun also spun in the air near the ceiling. Stretching out from the doors were three more of the unsettling, humanoid stains.

"What happened here? Do you think there was a cargo hold hull breach, and they were trying to seal it off?" Yama-moto asked, slipping around her captain to drift closer.

Tiggy's arm hair rose, and she choked back a command for the Medical Officer to retreat. Instead, she forced herself to approach while paging Cornell.

"Cornell, any evidence of a hull breach in cargo?" she asked.

There was a long moment of static over the comms line before her Engineering Officer finally answered.

"None. There's even oxygen, and the life support systems are functioning correctly. But, Captain, uh, we haven't found any bodies, but there have been some weird... stains?" Cornell replied.

Tiggy's skin prickled from her scalp down to her toes. "Heard. Stay in your suits, regardless of the current atmosphere, and send Stag back to the airlock. Meet Yamamoto and me at the cargo hold ASAP."

Yamamoto drifted to the control panel by the right of the doors. She tapped it a few times, then looked at Tiggy, shaking her head.

"It's been trashed, looks like they really wanted to keep the doors shut," she said.

Tiggy bumped against the cargo hold doors, hands gripping bent bolts on each to hold herself steady. Angling her head, she pointed her light through the narrow aperture, revealing a few towering crates strapped to the floor of the hold. Based on the value of the cargo they'd been sent to receive, Tiggy would guess it had been the last to be loaded and would be located closest to the external doors.

"We'll have to wait for Cornell, he might be able to manually open them," she said, pushing back away from the doors.

"Captain?"

Tiggy started, glad Yamamoto didn't see her flinch as she answered her comms.

"Greer, did you find anything in the black box data? We haven't seen a single body yet," she said.

"No critical occurrences, but there was a divergence from their course due to a mechanical issue. They landed on that nearby planet, Company data labels it as NS-8890," Greer replied.

NS meant "non-supportive of human life" and, since it was given a number rather than a name, meant it held no valuable resources.

"What kind of mechanical failure?" Tiggy asked, watching her Medical Officer take photos of the three stains around the cargo door, one of which was nearer the ceiling, where the bolt gun was.

"Nothing major, their starboard thruster backfired and caused some damage to the hull. The captain made a note that he felt – because of the fragile nature of the cargo – it would be better to land and repair rather than risk further complications."

Tiggy nodded to herself. She would have made the same call. The Company didn't respond kindly to those who risked its profits.

"This had to have been shortly before the distress call went out, considering the Ironside is not more than a day's flight away from the planet," she said over comms.

"Yes'm. About twenty-three hours after they left NS-8890. No indication of common critical occurrences logged though."

Cornell swept into view, coming around the corner, and Tiggy saw his eyes widening at the sight.

"I'll keep reading through the logs for anything unusual," Greer added, already sounding distracted.

"Thank you. We'll try and get this done all in one trip. I don't want to be on this ship any longer than we have to," Tiggy responded and nodded at Cornell. "Can you get those doors open?"

"Shit, Cap, I can try," he said and jumped off a wall, pulling himself to a stop in front of an access panel close to the floor.

The Captain was afraid it would take a while but after

only a few minutes, the gears squealed as they pulled the doors apart, revealing the cargo hold.

"I thought you turned on the lights?" she said, peering into the darkness.

"There must be an electrical malfunction." Her Engineering Officer shrugged, pushing away from the panel.

Tiggy floated in front of the doorway, turning her light this way and that, trying to spot any kind of movement.

"Captain?" Yamamoto bumped into her side, hooking her arm with Tiggy's so they floated together.

"Alright. The bounty should be at the very back. I'll go in and begin throwing the boxes. Yamamoto, you catch and throw down the corridor to Cornell, who'll pass it to Stag. Got it?"

She kicked into the cargo hold, leaving her companions and the light behind, as she navigated through the immense crates. Tiggy guessed she was nearing the back when a humming sound penetrated through her helmet and she could see a faint blue light ahead of her. The Captain kicked off the side of a crate, angled downward, and came into view of four refrigerated units tied to the floor. Domed with transparent covers, they pulsed coldly, filled with layers upon layers, rows upon rows, of human eggs – ready for implant.

The egg industry was one of the Company's most profitable, and these four boxes – each merely the size of the personal footlocker – were worth trillions of dollars.

But something was wrong.

Two of the units looked damaged. Tiggy pushed off another crate and drifted down to the egg carriers. She went to the intact units first, unlatching them from the floor, and giving them a gentle push to send them upwards. Then she examined the next unit. Its cover had been split up in ragged shards, compromising the product. The cold air manufactured by the internal refrigerator system seeped out from the destroyed lid, spiralling through the air like ghostly galaxies.

Tiggy peered inside. The eggs floated in tiny vials filled with synthetic amniotic fluid. What eggs were left, that is. Most of the vials were broken, their eggs gone, the liquid in free-floating drops above the chest, bouncing off Tiggy's helmet.

"Dammit," she said.

Likely this would result in a reduced bounty prize. She checked the other one and saw the same. Split tubes, missing eggs. Only half the product was still good. Her trip to Euphoria would have to wait a little longer. Tiggy kicked upward, grabbing a handle on each of the two units that could still be retrieved, as she hooked a foot on a crate's protruding railing and pulled her and the boxes forward, towards the exit.

Guiding the boxes, Tiggy frowned and looked over her shoulder. She had originally thought that the humming she heard had come from the refrigeration mechanism within the egg storage units, but it was still coming from behind her, rather than from either side, from the boxes she pushed.

The dark cargo bay still looked empty, but the humming intensified, making her teeth ache. Shaking her head, Tiggy turned back to the interior doors. She could see Yamamoto waiting at the first hall junction, and the Medical Officer gave a little wave.

"Captain, I've got to the end of the black box data

and…" the normally stoic Greer trailed off, sounding unsure.

"What is it, Greer?"

"I don't think the Company wanted us to find this," Greer replied, almost whispering, as if the Company were eavesdropping. "The last message from the captain of the Ironside. They sent back a scrubber, but the connection to Vulpes server was cut before the job could finish. Uh, the message is pretty fragmented, but here it is: 'This is Captain Abernathy. I have an emergency.' There's a bunch of gibberish, then it goes: 'Cargo corruption, likely due to the strange frequencies NS-8890 was giving off.' Then: 'premature growth and unnatural mutation. Please send permission to eject all cargo for safety of crew. Three dead already.' And the rest is gibberish."

"What the hell does that mean?" Tiggy said, looking first at the egg box she held with her right hand, then to the left.

Ahead of her, Yamamoto dropped her hand and kicked forward, towards the Captain. Behind Tiggy, something began to scream.

Moments became snapshots, carefully separated, individual from one another.

Tiggy realized that whatever the hell was screaming behind her was something Yamamoto felt she needed to save Tiggy from. Which meant it was something dangerous. Tiggy also realized that no matter how sexy Yamamoto would look in a black bikini in a hot spring pool on Euphoria, it wasn't worth their lives.

The next moment: the screamer was joined by another, and another. Tiggy released her grip on the left unit.

The moment after: she swung the right unit around and

behind her, bracing her feet against it, keeping her eyes on Yamamoto. She kicked off.

Launching off an unanchored item only gave her a small boost, but it allowed Tiggy to speed up, and she reached for Yamamoto's outstretched hand. The Medical Officer, gripping the edge of the massive cargo bay door, yanked the Captain through the threshold and flung her down the hall. Caught off balance, Tiggy flipped around and watched Yamamoto leap towards her.

Beyond the Medical Officer, in the cargo bay, something pulsed with a strange light that gave Tiggy an instant headache. Figures, immune to the lack of gravity, ran towards the officers along the polycarb floor. Strange humanoid figures – or rather the suggestion of human figures.

Their shapes were defined by two identical silhouettes overlapped, one in violet light and one in copper light. The result was a painful visual experience similar to the anaglyphic technique created by primitive humans to mimic a 3D stereo effect – kiloyears before the invention of holograms. Tiggy's stomach roiled against the visual assault as she activated her comms.

"Greer, prime airlock to disengage for immediate evacuation. Everyone: we are aborting the mission. Abort!" she screamed, hoping they could hear her over the howling coming from the cargo bay.

The shrieks pounded against her eardrums in the same way the eerie figures assaulted her eyes. Someone else was shouting over the comms, but she couldn't hear the words, she couldn't understand them. Her fear was slowing down time again, stuttering it.

"Akemi!" Tiggy screamed, holding out her gloved hand to Yamamoto.

The Captain counted three dozen figures swarming out of the cargo bay, screaming in a strange harmony. This close, she could tell that they were smaller than the average adult – more the size of teenagers – running in a stilted manner, hands reaching.

Tiggy slammed against the wall where the corridor forked and instinctively reached behind her to grab a strut. Akemi's hand came within range and, bracing her boots against the wall, Tiggy grabbed her and threw her around the corner, into the corridor in the airlock's direction. Flexing her arms, Tiggy swung around to follow and collided with Cornell.

They bounced off one another, Tiggy flailing about in a somersault before hitting the ceiling and him back to the floor. The polychromatic light crept around the corner of the corridor, brighter than the overhead lights, heralding the approach of the spectres. Cornell pulled himself up and pointed his lasgun. His mouth was moving but, even though the comms speaker fed right into her helmet, Tiggy could barely hear him.

"What the hell is it? What's going on?" Was the most she heard.

"Retreat, Cornell! Retreat!" she screamed as the flood arrived.

First was the light, then the screams cresting into a stampede of those things that surrounded Cornell. The lasgun fired over and over again, flashes of light darting through the figures and singing the wall instead.

One of them reached out and grabbed the Engineering Officer's shoulder. Cornell seized up, his head thrown back as he began to shake. He convulsed, his head slamming into the wall. Other beings grabbed at his thrashing limbs, and his body vibrated so hard that the edges blurred. The figures piled on, wrapping their ethereal limbs around him, draping him in embraces.

Tiggy thought she could hear his screams separate from theirs. Then the entities went silent and still. One by one, almost politely, they climbed off one another. Cornell was gone, with only a new seven-foot-tall human-shaped shadow burned into the polycarb to commemorate his life.

The sight shocked Tiggy back to herself, and she launched off, speeding through the air. She caught up to Yamamoto quickly, the Medical Officer had kept going but slowly, obviously waiting for the Captain and Engineering Officer.

"Dammit, Cornell." Tiggy swallowed back a sob. "Why weren't you back in the airlock like I ordered?"

"Captain?" Yamamoto said, but Tiggy only shook her head.

The screams began again. First one, then three, then dozens. The hunt renewed.

Tiggy and Yamamoto had a speed advantage, launching themselves off the walls and ceiling, whipping through the narrow corridors of the Ironside until the airlock came into view. Tiggy's heart dropped. The door should have been open.

The two women slammed into it. Stag was on the other side, fumbling with the panel.

"Stag, open the door. Open it!" Tiggy shouted into her

comms, hearing her voice crack, letting the fear through.

The Logistics Officer turned and looked at her, his cheeks smeared with tears, his moustache drenched with snot.

"I heard him! I heard him die screaming, Captain!" he babbled between sobs and he clutched his head, sinking to his knees.

Tiggy slammed the heel of her fist against the door. "Greer! Open the airlock, Yamamoto and I are trapped in the Ironside!"

The screams flowed down the hall, bizarre copper and violet light slunk down, painting the walls and ceiling with an eye-stinging effect.

"I can't, Captain! Stag's overridden external commands—"

Greer's voice was drowned out by the screams of the colour-tortured souls that neared. Tiggy grabbed Yamamoto's hand and pulled her away from the airlock door, they darted down the opposite passageway, towards the bow of the Ironside. The corridor curved with the shape of the hull.

Tiggy whispered prayers to the stars under her breath.

She prayed until she saw the next airlock door, which was open.

Yanking Yamamoto around in a painful arc, Tiggy flung them both inside the airlock. Still gripping the Medical Officer's hand, she typed in her code to initiate the decompression sequence. The airlock door closed slowly. The sinister polychromatic light rushed over the wall opposite the door and Yamamoto screamed into the comms, clinging to the Captain.

The mutants of light and colour appeared and one flung

out its arm between the door and the frame. The door shut, slicing through the arm.

The amputated limb fell to the floor, despite the lack of gravity, and burned a gray shadow of itself into the material as it faded to nothing.

The air hissed out, the airlock door window was filled with the violet and copper light of death, but Tiggy turned away from it. Now that the sound was gone, she could think again. She could hear Yamamoto sobbing through comms. The external door lights changed from yellow to red, opening to the vast void of space. Tiggy pulled a cable from her belt, clipping herself to the Medical Officer. Then she stepped to the edge of the external airlock door.

She risked a look over her shoulder.

The things had begun to pry open the airlock door, much as they had the cargo bay door, and she wouldn't bet any money they needed air to survive. Turning back, the two women swung out, Tiggy gripping an external hand mount, Yamamoto holding Tiggy's hand and trusting in her completely.

The Captain used her momentum to fling Yamamoto out into the emptiness of space, towards the Claymore. The cable from her belt spooled out, sending vibrations through Tiggy's waist until there was a jerk as it reached its end, and she was yanked away from the Ironside's hull just as Yamamoto grabbed one of the external handholds on the Claymore's side. Swinging wide, Tiggy hit a button on her belt and felt another jerk as the cable began to respool, taking her swiftly towards Yamamoto.

"Greer, open cargo's external door, Yamamoto and I are

boarding," she shouted into her comms.

Her remaining Engineering Officer didn't reply, but Greer didn't need to because the Claymore's small cargo door began to open. Spiderlike, Yamamoto crawled across the hull, pulling Tiggy with her.

The Captain looked behind her. The anaglyphic specters spilled out of the airlock, dozens of them, brilliant ghastly stars in the void of space. A shuddering chill sunk into Tiggy's bones. They were even unaffected by space. The beings swam through the nothingness, straight for the Claymore.

"Fuck," Tiggy sobbed, then opened her comms again. "Greer, be ready for immediate FTL!"

"Captain, that would destroy the Ironside –"

"Greer!" Tiggy was only vaguely aware she was screaming. "Prep FTL! The threat is in pursuit!"

Her scream turned into one of pain rather than fear, as she clipped the edge of the cargo bay door on her way in. She heard her femur snap as much as felt it, whipping past Yamamoto, who clung to a box of freeze-dried rations.

"Close the cargo door and go, Greer! Go!" Tiggy howled through the pain and slammed into the hull.

"Everyone, hold on, this'll be rough!" came Greer's response.

Not even fully open, the cargo door began to close again. The beings formed a wall of light, vibrating with an intensity that burned into Tiggy's brain, even after she clenched her eyes shut in terror. She felt the engines kick into high gear. Something collided with her, and Tiggy screamed, struggling, before she saw it was Yamamoto.

"I got you, Tigs, I got you!" Yamamoto said, reaching

around the Captain and gripping the netting behind them, entangling them in it.

The cargo door shut a fraction of a second before FTL engaged, and the two women were wrenched violently against the netting as the Claymore shot away. But even as Tiggy was carried away, light-years and light-years in seconds, she thought she could hear their screams – the screams of those blighted by colour and light – in the shriek of the FTL drive. Clutching Yamamoto tighter, Tiggy decided that she would find a way to make the trip to Euphoria work and she would be taking Yamamoto with her.

ACKNOWLEDGMENTS

Thank you to Solomon Forse, for crumbling under my insistence he write my foreword. And Molly Collins who did the formatting and cover layout, turning my chaos into a fine looking collection.

And the biggest thank you to my husband, Matt, whose support made all this possible. He has sat through many meals where I have pitched newly fledged ideas at him – and a lot of those times, he was still able to point out possible plot holes I'd missed. He is my spaceship architect and detailed description demander. He keeps me going.

Also thanks to my cats, Poe and Zerg, who terrorize me every day.

P.L. McMillan is a writer whose works have been known to cause rifts in time and space itself…

Well, not quite. But writing often makes her feel that powerful.

With a passion for cosmic horror and sci-fi horror, P.L. McMillan sees every shadow as an entryway to a deeper look into the black heart of the world, meant to be discovered and explored. Infatuated with the works of Shirley Jackson, H.P. Lovecraft, and Ridley Scott, her dream is to create stories of adventure, of chills, of heartbreak, and thrills.

P.L. McMillan lives in Colorado, with her large selection of teas, her husband, and her two chinchillas (Sherlock and Spuds) – all under the supervision of their black cat overlords, Poe and Zerg.

Find her on her website: https://www.plmcmillan.com/
Or on Twitter: @authorplm

Printed in Great Britain
by Amazon